I0635845

Hitchhiking from Fort Lewis

& Other Stories

Rocket Science Press
SHIPWRECKT BOOKS PUBLISHING COMPANY
Winona, Minnesota

Hitchhiking from Fort Lewis

& Other Stories

Daryl Lanz

Cover and Interior Design by Shipwreckt Books
Cover image of hitchhiking veterans was created using equal
measures of Shutterstock AI and Affinity Photo and Design Software.

Shipwreckt Books Publishing Company
357 W. Wabasha Street
Winona, Minnesota 55987

Library of Congress Control Number: 2024938651

To the memory of my mother, Phyllis, who read to me as a child and instilled in me a love of stories and reading.

Contents

1. Hitchhiking from Fort Lewis

S tanding on the sidewalk, Kenny Landwirth watched the traffic. A truck rumbled by going one way and an army jeep the other. Kenny thought he recognized the soldier driving the jeep, but he kept his eyes on the road and didn't look toward Kenny.

Kenny took one last drag on his cigarette and squinted against the bright mid-morning sun. He dropped the cigarette to the sidewalk and ground it down with his heel. He'd have to quit this habit when he got home.

He turned and glanced through the window into the office behind him. Roy Flint, Kenny's army buddy, stood at the counter inside talking with the bus station clerk. Roy flung his arms wide, gesturing; the clerk simply stared at him, shaking his head. Like Kenny, Roy still wore his army uniform. It had been just over an hour since they'd received their discharge papers.

Kenny reached down and picked up his duffel bag from the sidewalk where it sat next to him. Roy came out of the bus station office.

"No dice," Roy said.

Kenny looked at him. "We can't get tickets?" he asked.

"No discounts for servicemen."

"So …?"

"Unless you want to pay full price. Which I don't. I want to get back home with money in my pocket." He patted his shirt pocket with his right hand. Kenny thought that was odd; he could tell that pocket was empty. "You got a girl waiting for you back home, right?" Roy continued.

Kenny wasn't sure there was a girl waiting for him back home. But he'd told the story so many times he'd come to believe it. "Yeah. I hope she's waiting for me," he said.

"Right. You don't want to show up with empty pockets." Kenny wanted another cigarette. He thought about asking Roy for one but didn't.

"Honorable discharge," Roy said. "Thanks for your service, boys. Off you go. Too fucking bad you've got two thousand miles to go to get back home. You're not in the army anymore, so it's not the army's problem. That's your SNAFU, all right."

Kenny wasn't sure home was two thousand miles away. Then again, he wasn't sure that it wasn't. In either case, he agreed with Roy's sentiment.

"Back to plan B, then?" Kenny asked.

"No. Plan B was getting the bus company to give us discounted tickets as discharged servicemen. Since that didn't work out, it's back to the original. Plan A."

"Hitchhiking."

"Hitchhiking. We save all our money, plus we can probably bum meals off whoever gives us rides."

Kenny nodded. He wasn't sure he liked the idea of hitchhiking halfway across the country, but Roy was adamant that it would work. Plus, what did he have to be worried about? They were soldiers; discharged, sure, but still in uniform. That should help them get rides. And they'd been trained in combat, so they should be safe. They could handle anything. Even if most of his time in the army had been spent under the hood of a jeep or driving one around.

"Let's move out, Tech Corporal," Roy said, turning away and leading Kenny down the sidewalk.

The two men waited on the side of the road for only ten minutes before a pickup pulled over. The truck was a 1940 Ford that at one time had been red, but now most of the paint had flaked off. The driver leaned across the seat, removed a toothpick from his mouth, and called out the window.

"You boys looking for a ride?"

Roy stepped closer and leaned in the open window. "Yes, sir, we sure are."

"Where you headed?"

"Well, sir," Roy replied, as he reached up and scratched his head. "We're on our way back home to the Midwest." The driver let out a long, low whistle.

"That's a mighty long trip ahead of ya."

"Yes, sir, we know it."

"Well, I'm going most of the way across Washington, to Walla Walla. Climb on in."

"Thanks," Roy said. He tossed his duffel bag over the wooden boards (also once painted red but now faded) that bracketed the pickup's bed. Kenny did the same, then climbed into the cab behind Roy who slid over next to the driver.

"I'm Roy Flint," he introduced himself. "This is Kenny Landwirth."

"Bud Norris," the old man said. He pulled a fresh toothpick from his shirt pocket and placed it between his teeth. Bud pulled back onto the highway. "You boys on leave?" he asked.

"No, sir," Roy answered. "We got our discharge papers this morning."

"Well, congratulations. I served from '24 'til '27."

"Army?"

"Yep. Made it to Corporal."

"Roy here's a Corporal," Kenny chimed in. As soon as he said it, he realized he should have used the past tense. Roy had been a Corporal that morning, but now, like Kenny, he was another civilian.

"Is that right?" Bud sounded impressed.

"Yes, sir," Roy answered. "Got my promotion about a month ago."

"How about you, Kenny? What rank were you?"

Roy answered before Kenny could speak. "Kenny's a Tech Corporal."

"Tech Corporal?" Bud asked. "What's that?"

"Technician Fifth Grade," Kenny answered him. "That's the official rank."

"But it's essentially the same rank as Corporal," Roy insisted. "That's why we all called him Tech Corporal."

"Well, that's a new one for me," Bud said. "Didn't have that in my day."

Bud drove on in silence for a while. Roy leaned his head back against the seat and closed his eyes. Kenny looked out the window, watched as the trees rolled by.

"You boys see any action?" Bud asked after some time. Kenny looked over at him. He hoped Roy would answer, but Roy kept his eyes closed. Kenny doubted Roy was asleep, but it fell on him to answer.

"No, we didn't. I got drafted near the end of '45. The war was over before Roy and I joined the army."

Roy snorted at the word "joined" and Kenny knew then that he wasn't sleeping, that he was listening to the conversation. Neither Roy nor Kenny had enlisted on his own; both had been drafted. Roy liked to make that clear. Kenny thought it best to continue on.

"The closest we ever came to leaving the country was going out on a big boat in the Pacific one time."

"Navy boat?" Bud asked.

"Yeah, I guess so. I don't really know."

Roy had opened his eyes and was watching the highway unfold in front of them as the truck rumbled along, but he stayed silent and let Kenny tell the story.

"Where'd you go?" Bud said.

"Sir?"

"The navy boat. Where'd it take you?"

"Oh. Well, we had kind of a—a simulated landing they called it. Took us down the coast to California and we came onshore like we were landing in another country, I guess. That's the only time I ever been on a ship like that. Just down the coast to California."

"Then what?"

"They put us on a train back to Fort Lewis."

Bud nodded but didn't say anything more. Kenny tried to catch Roy's eye, but Roy just kept looking out the windshield at the highway. Kenny turned away, looking out the side window at the trees and fields they were driving past. He had come to Washington on the train from Minnesota, but he hadn't spent much of that time looking at the scenery. He didn't think he'd ever been more than one hundred miles away from home before—hell, probably not more than fifty—and he was scared and homesick. After he arrived at Fort Lewis and the routine set in, he felt better, but he wondered about the area around the base. And right now, he wanted just to look out the window and not have to think. They drove in silence for most of the day. Only when Roy marveled at the scenery did Bud speak up. He told them they were passing through the eastern edge of Mt. Ranier National Park. "Founded in 1899. One of the first national parks in the country."

"Beautiful," Roy whispered.

"Sure is," Bud said.

Kenny couldn't tear his gaze away from watching the trees and rolling hillsides out the window. It reminded him a bit of home, but the trees here were different. Pines, he knew, rather than deciduous. He could see snow-capped mountains nearby.

"Supposed to be the snowiest place on earth," Bud said. "Leastways that's what I heard."

Kenny wondered about that. Plenty of snow fell back home in Minnesota. Still, it was summer now and he could see snow on the mountaintops. He didn't see that back home.

They drove down highway 410, through the towns of Yakima, Buena, and Zilah. When they reached a place called Sunnyside, Bud pulled over for a "rest stop." Before getting back in the truck, Bud said, "We still got about one hundred miles to go to get ta Walla Walla. I could drive it myself if I had to, but I'm getting mighty tired. Wouldn't mind if one of you boys took over for a while."

"I'd be happy to," Roy told him. "I spent most of my time in the service chauffeuring officers here and there. Driving's kind of second nature to me."

"I surely do 'preciate it," Bud said. "If I doze off, just stay on 410."

Roy nodded and climbed in behind the wheel. Kenny slid over to the center and Bud took his spot on the right side of the cab. They weren't on the road ten minutes before Bud was snoring away.

Kenny and Roy talked quietly as they drove on, mostly about what they planned to do when they got back home. Roy had dreams of starting his own trucking service and marrying his high school sweetheart. Kenny wasn't sure about his future. His older brother had taken over the family farm from their dad, who still lived in the old farmhouse and helped out where he could, though his knees and shoulders bothered him most days. Kenny had started driving a milk delivery truck with a friend but got drafted a month or so later. Maybe he could go back to that.

They passed more towns with odd-sounding names like Kiona, Kennewick, and Wallula. After that last one, the highway ran alongside the Walla Walla River, and they figured they must be getting close.

Later that evening, well after dark, Kenny found himself sharing the backseat of a 1946 Plymouth with Roy. Roy sat behind the driver, a man named Dave Taubner, who was just a few years older than Kenny and Roy. Dave's wife, Betty Lou, sat in front of Kenny.

Kenny kept drifting off to sleep, lulled by the conversation between Roy and Dave, and the smooth, steady motion of the Plymouth along the highway. He had been awake since 0530 hours—5:30 a.m., he had to remind himself to readjust to civilian life. Dave had served in the war in Europe but spoke of it only in hushed tones. Still, Roy was impressed, Kenny could tell. Kenny had always been thankful the war had ended before he'd been drafted.

When they met the occasional car headed west, its headlights lit up the Plymouth's interior for a moment. Kenny's eyes were drawn to Betty Lou, her shoulder length brunette hair pushed back from her forehead by a green knit headband. Betty Lou watched her husband, but Kenny noticed that she looked back at Roy quite a bit as she followed their conversation. She smiled at Roy's feeble jokes—Kenny had heard them all before. He wondered if Dave didn't notice that Roy flirted with his wife or if he just ignored it. She wasn't a great beauty, but she was pretty, so maybe Dave was used to it.

When they had reached Walla Walla, Bud had directed Roy to stop at a diner where he bought them all dinner. Kenny ordered pork chops while Bud and Roy both had the prime rib special. A full meal and several cups of coffee later, the three men sat talking. The Taubners, in the next booth, overheard some of the conversation, and Dave introduced himself. The couple was headed home to Lewiston, Idaho, that night and offered to drive Roy and Kenny ("fellow vets," Dave called them) that far. The sun had set by the time they left Walla Walla.

Kenny came awake suddenly. The car still glided through the night. It was dark. Dave drummed his fingers on the steering wheel and sang softly to himself. Betty Lou's head rested against his shoulder. Kenny glanced at Roy; he might have been asleep, or he might have been looking out the window into the darkness. Lights in the distance ahead showed they were approaching a city.

Kenny cleared his throat. "Where are we?" he asked.

"Welcome back to the land of the living," Dave joked. "I was beginning to think you'd sleep all the way there."

"Sorry," Kenny murmured. He felt oddly embarrassed, but he didn't know why.

"Don't worry," Dave said. "You deserve the rest. I know what it's like the day you get your release from Uncle Sam's glorious brotherhood. But to answer your question, we're just coming up on Clarkston."

"Clarkston?"

"Clarkston, Washington. Lewiston's sister city, or her little sister, as I like to call it. We drive through Clarkston, cross the Snake River, and bam, we're back home in Lewiston."

"Lewis and Clark," Roy piped up; he was awake after all. "They sure admire those two out here, don't they?"

Back home in Minnesota, Kenny lived just down the road from a town named Lewiston. He didn't think "his" Lewiston was named after the famous explorer, but he wasn't sure. He thought about saying something, but the others were continuing their conversation, and he didn't want to interrupt.

Dave laughed at Roy's comment. "Lots of stuff named after them, that's for sure."

Betty Lou sat up. The men's talk woke her. "Are we almost home?"

"Sure are, honey. Just coming into Clarkston."

"What time is it?"

Dave looked at his watch. Now that they were passing through town, just enough light illuminated the interior of the car so he could see it. "Going on midnight," he said.

"We really do appreciate the ride," Roy said.

Kenny wondered what they'd do next. Midnight in Lewiston, Idaho. Getting another ride east at this hour seemed unlikely. Dave answered his unspoken question.

"You two can stay the night with us. The accommodations aren't much, but we'd be happy to have you."

"I can make up the couch for one of you," Betty Lou said. "The other one might have to sleep on the floor."

"That sounds just fine, Betty," Roy said.

"Thank you," Kenny added.

"Betty Lou can make you a big breakfast in the morning," Dave said. "Bet it's been a while since you've had a home-cooked meal. And Betty Lou's a fine cook. I suppose you'll want to make an early start tomorrow, get back on the road."

"I suppose we will," Roy said.

Kenny noticed that Roy was looking at Betty Lou when he said it, and she was looking back at him. "Right," Kenny said. "We've still got a long ways to go to get home."

The Taubners' house was cozy and warm. A couch and matching easy chair with an ottoman filled up most of the small living room. The radio stood in one corner. Betty Lou had made lacy curtains that hung in front of the long windows. Dave switched on the one lamp in the room. Roy looked admiringly at a framed watercolor landscape— mountains, trees, a stream—that hung over the couch.

"Betty Lou painted that herself," Dave said, pride in his voice. "I made the frame."

"It's lovely," Roy said. Kenny didn't think he'd ever heard Roy use that word before.

Betty Lou brought a sheet and some blankets from the other room. Roy used the bathroom, and Kenny sat in the chair while Betty Lou made up the couch. Kenny didn't know if he should offer to help or just sit there and wait. Dave returned from the basement with a sleeping bag that he tossed to Kenny, who spread it out on the floor, grateful for something to do.

"I'm beat, fellas," Dave said. "I need to hit the hay before I collapse."

Kenny thought it odd that Dave used the word "fellas" when only he and Betty Lou were in the room, though he supposed Roy could maybe hear them through the bathroom door.

Betty Lou handed Kenny a pillow. Roy came out of the bathroom, passing Dave in the hallway. They exchanged good nights.

"All the comforts of home," Roy said, smiling at Betty Lou.

"It's not much," she said. "But I hope you both will be comfortable."

"It's wonderful," Roy said. He looked like he wanted to say something more. He and Betty Lou stared at each other for a moment.

"Thank you," Kenny said, breaking the uncomfortable silence. Betty Lou smiled at Kenny, then she turned and left the room.

"Couch or floor?" Roy asked.

"You can take the couch," Kenny said.

"You sure?"

Kenny nodded. Roy plopped down on the couch and unlaced his boots.

Kenny went off to the bathroom. He brushed his teeth and looked at his reflection in the mirror. The harsh fluorescent light in the bathroom left him looking haggard. He rubbed his chin and cheeks. He needed a shave.

When he returned to the living room, Roy was sacked out on the couch, his back to the room. Kenny stripped down to his underwear and undershirt, then turned off the lamp and lay down on the floor. After dozing in the car on the drive from Walla Walla, Kenny lay awake for a long time before finally falling asleep. He woke once during the night, the room dark but for the moonlight seeping through the windows. Roy wasn't on the couch. After a moment, Kenny heard the toilet flush and light from the bathroom flooded into the living room for a second before the switch was flicked off. Roy shuffled back to the couch and lay down.

What seemed like less than a minute later, the light came back on. Kenny saw Betty Lou's figure silhouetted in the bathroom doorway. She wore a dark nightgown that ended around the knees. Her arms were bare. Kenny thought she looked into the living room for a moment before closing the bathroom door behind her.

When Kenny woke next it was to the smell of coffee brewing. Early morning sunlight streamed through the windows. Roy stirred on the couch, but continued snoring. Kenny took his pants and shirt into the bathroom where he dressed. When he returned to the living room, Roy was gone, but Kenny heard hushed voices coming from the kitchen. He found Roy sitting at a small Formica-covered table sipping coffee from a ceramic mug while Betty Lou, dressed in a long white robe, fried potatoes on the stove.

"Morning, Tech Corporal," Roy said.

Betty Lou turned from the stove when she heard Roy speak. "Good morning, Kenny. Did you sleep well? Or at least okay on that hard floor?"

"Good morning, Mrs. Taubner. I slept just fine, thank you."

"Well, I'm glad for that. And it's Betty Lou, please." She turned back to the stove.

Kenny breathed in deeply. The smell of frying potatoes reminded him of home.

"Would you like a cup of coffee, Kenny? Help yourself." Betty Lou indicated a coffeemaker on the counter. An empty cup sat next to it.

"Thank you, ma'am—Betty Lou," Kenny said.

Kenny sat down next to Roy. They talked about where to go next while Betty Lou finished cooking their breakfast. Roy watched Betty Lou carefully. She had thin arms and long fingers. Kenny made note of the wedding band encircling one of them. Her robe ended shortly above her ankles— Kenny appreciated a well-turned ankle—and her feet were tucked into fuzzy slippers.

Betty Lou dished the potatoes onto two plates and added a couple of fried eggs to each. (She had fried the eggs quickly while Roy and Kenny talked.) She set the plates on the table in front of the two men and sat next to Kenny, across the table from Roy.

"None for you?" Kenny asked.

Betty Lou shook her head. "I'm fine with just coffee for now. You fellas dig in."

Roy was chewing a large forkful of potatoes. "This is delicious," he managed to say. Kenny grunted in agreement. She had added some chopped-up onions to the potatoes, which added a tartness to the flavor.

"What about Dave?" Roy asked, reaching for his coffee.

"He's sleeping in, after our long day yesterday. I'll make him breakfast later. I figured you boys wanted to get on the road early." Roy nodded, bringing another forkful of potatoes to his mouth.

"Dave was in the Army in Europe? During the war?" Kenny asked.

Betty Lou parted her lips to answer, but Roy spoke first. "We talked about this last night, Kenny, in the car. I guess you were asleep then."

"I did doze off for a bit." Kenny felt embarrassed again, still not sure why.

"He saw some action," Betty Lou said quietly, "but he doesn't talk about it. Sometimes I find him just sitting with his eyes kind of glazed over, staring off into nothing, you know. And once in a while at night, he'll wake up screaming. It frightens me."

Roy nodded. "Shellshock," he said. Roy and Kenny had heard about it back on base. Soldiers who had come back from combat, but couldn't get over it, couldn't adjust to being back in the normal, everyday world again.

The men finished eating and talked about where they were heading next, east through Idaho to Montana. Betty Lou fetched some paper and sketched out a crude map. "Spalding's the next town over," she said. "Then there's a couple more small towns here and here—" She made x's on the map—"Sorry I don't know all the names. Dave and I moved out here from Pennsylvania after we finished high school, and then he got drafted almost right away. I was pretty much on my own, didn't know anyone in town really, and no relatives close by."

"That must have been rough," Roy said sympathetically.

Betty Lou shrugged. "I got by okay. Joined a church. That helped me get to know some of the ladies."

"So when we get to Montana, where do we go?" Kenny asked.

"I suppose you want to head for Missoula," Betty Lou said. "I think there's a pretty good road through the mountains that ends up there." She shook her head. "Someone on the road will surely know more than me."

"We sure do appreciate all your hospitality, Betty Lou," Roy said, smiling. "That was a wonderful breakfast."

"Just glad I could help," she said, looking down. Kenny thought she was blushing.

Kenny stood up. "Give our thanks to your husband, ma'am," he said.

As they walked down the road away from the Taubners' house, Roy whistled. "That sure was nice."

Kenny nodded in agreement. "Yep. Good food, a place to sleep. I'm feeling good this morning."

"And what about that Betty Lou? What a looker."

"She is pretty," Kenny said. "Married woman, though."

"Doesn't mean I can't look. And appreciate the view."

They caught a ride with an elderly minister to Spalding. Kenny hoped that would help turn Roy's thinking away from Betty Lou Taubner. After that, a middle-aged couple drove them through a town called Myrtle and dropped them off in one called Orofino. They waited there on the side of the road for over an hour before an old farmer—he could have been Bud's twin brother—in a pickup pulled over and offered them a ride. "Going as far as Pierce," he said.

Neither Roy nor Kenny had any idea how far that was, but they tossed their bags in the back and climbed into the cab. Just before getting to a town named Weippe, the road changed from blacktop to gravel. Kenny was used to gravel roads—heck, lots of the roads he traveled on his milk delivery route back in Minnesota weren't paved—but he started to wonder if they were getting off track. Maybe this wasn't the best road to get where they were going. He figured they had a few more days of travel ahead of them and hoped the going wouldn't be too rough. But from Weippe to Pierce the road was paved again, and he felt better.

The feeling didn't last. Mid-afternoon the two men were jammed into the cab of a logging truck driven by a burly man named Aaron. He had tattoos covering both forearms ("from my days in the navy") and an unkempt beard that hung nearly to his stomach. On leaving Pierce, he told them he could take them as far as Lolo, Montana, though the road through the east Idaho mountains wasn't paved. It was, as they discovered, in fact, dirt. The truck rumbled along this path, and at times, the edge of the road (Kenny, sitting on the right side, could see through the open window) dropped off precipitously without guard rails or any kind of protection. Kenny felt his stomach rise and fall. He felt queasy and dizzy. He tried closing his eyes, but that only made it worse. With every bump and lurch he clenched his fists tighter.

"You gents are headed to Wisconsin?" Aaron asked. Roy nodded. Kenny was looking out the window and stayed silent.

"I am," Roy said. "Kenny here's from Minnesota."

"And you came out of Fort Lewis back in Washington?"

"That's right."

Aaron chuckled. "Well, I hope you're enjoying the view. You might have come the wrong way."

"How's that?"

"If you'd stayed north in Washington up to Spokane, you would have crossed to Coeur d'Alene, then dropped down to Missoula from there. Or taken the Roosevelt Highway. That goes all the way through to Wisconsin, I think. Better roads."

"Better than this?" Roy joked.

Aaron's laugh was deep and hearty. "Don't worry none. You're safe with me. Been through this way dozens of times."

Kenny looked away from the window at the big man. "That's good to know. This probably isn't as dangerous as it looks."

Aaron drew a deep breath and let it out slowly. "We're coming up on a spot where a truck went over the edge last fall. I'll point it out to you." His voice got quieter. The mood in the cab darkened.

"Did the driver ... survive?" Roy asked.

"Nope."

Kenny looked back out the window. They were on a fairly level stretch of road, trees lined on either side close to the edge. Around a curve, the road rose quickly and steeply. The mountains rose on Kenny's side, crowding the edge of the road. On the other side of the narrow path was the drop-off. Aaron kept the truck steady down the center of the road.

Kenny wondered what would happen if another truck came from the other direction. Could they possibly even pass one another here?

Aaron seemed relaxed. Kenny felt like he was going to throw up, but he didn't. Roy's face was a mask. They continued along the dirt road highway through the mountains, although it took most of the day, coming at last to the Lolo Pass on the Idaho-Montana border. At the pass, the highest point they'd reached, snow still lined the sides of the road. Lewis and Clark had come through this pass on their journey to the west, and the Nez Perce Indians had used it before that. Aaron told all this to Roy and Kenny as they approached the pass.

"Only about 40 more miles to Missoula," Aaron said as they crested the pass. Once they started down the Montana side, the road improved slightly, but it was still only gravel all the way to the town of Lolo, Aaron's final destination. When they arrived in Lolo ("Another place Lewis and Clark camped out" according to Aaron), he directed them to highway 93. "It's only about a half hour's drive to Missoula from here," he told them.

Roy and Kenny thanked him for bringing them over the mountains and into Lolo. He wished them good luck and within 15 minutes, they were picked up by a young man in his thirties, a geology professor at the University of Montana in Missoula. The professor drove them into Missoula and dropped them off at a roadside motel just after crossing the Clark Fork River.

The cost of the motel wasn't much, but it was an expense that Roy and Kenny hadn't counted on. If they'd taken the bus from Ft. Lewis, they would have been able to sleep on it as they traveled overnight. They paid for a room with two single beds and got up early in the morning to get back on the road. They bought breakfast—bacon, eggs, and coffee— at a small diner in Missoula, then headed to the west side of town. There they caught a ride with a U.S. Forest Service ranger on his way to Butte. They headed out of Missoula on Highway 10.

"I'm really not supposed to pick up hitchhikers," the ranger—his name was Brook—told them as soon as they climbed into his truck. "But for a couple of servicemen like yourselves I'll make an exception."

Both Kenny and Roy expressed their thanks.

"Unless, of course, the two of you are AWOL," he joked.

"No sir," Roy answered him. "We were discharged two days ago."

"Just trying to make our way back home," Kenny added.

"And where's home?" Brook asked.

"Minnesota for me," Kenny told him. "Roy here's from Wisconsin."

"Rhinelander, Wisconsin," Roy said.

"Can't say as I know much about that part of the country," Brook said. "Born and raised here in Montana. Took my degree from the UM in Missoula and started on with the Forest Service the next year. Been with them ever since."

Kenny looked out the window at the pine forest and snow-capped mountains. "Beautiful country," he said.

"Sure is," Ranger Brook agreed. "Minnesota's pretty flat, ain't it?"

"Parts of it, I guess. Where I'm from there's a lot of bluffs, hills and valleys. Along the rivers. Nothing like these mountains, though."

"Nope. Ain't nothing like the Rockies."

The three men were quiet for a while as the truck rumbled down Highway 10. Kenny wondered if Roy would tell Brook about his hometown, Rhinelander—he'd talked about it sometimes back on base—but Roy didn't bring it up. After a moment, Brook asked, "How long were you two in the army?"

They told the story again about when they'd joined (or were drafted) and that they hadn't seen any "action" as the war was over before they were inducted. Kenny thought he'd better get used to telling this story whenever he met someone new once he got back home. Then Kenny told the story he'd told Bud about taking the boat down the California coast for the simulated landing. Ranger Brook seemed to like that story.

"I never served in the military," Brook told them as they passed through a town called Deer Lodge. "Went to the university straight out of high school. That was 1929. Guess I coulda joined up, but it didn't seem like such a big thing to me back then. Between the wars and all, I guess."

"I don't think you missed much," Roy said.

"How's that?"

"The army life," Roy said. He didn't say anything more. Kenny wondered what he meant.

"You must have learned some useful skills, though, didn't you?" Brook asked. "Something that'll serve you in civilian life."

Roy smiled. "I mostly drove officers around."

"Roy and I worked in the motor pool," Kenny said.

"Working on cars and such?" Brook asked. "Engines?"

"Yeah," Kenny nodded. "I guess I learned a lot about how to fix Jeep engines."

"Well, there you go. That's something that should help you out when you get back home. I know in the Forest Service a good mechanic's always a valuable asset."

Kenny thought about that. He hoped to go back to his milk delivery route when he got home. If that job was still waiting for him. He remembered times when the trucks broke down. That always caused a delay. Maybe now he'd be able to help a little more in that regard. Maybe his eighteen months in the army would prove useful after all.

Ranger Brook dropped them off when they reached Butte. "Stay on highway 10 heading east," he told them. "Good luck to you."

They thanked Brook, grabbed their packs, and started hitching again.

It wasn't long before a car pulled over to the side of the road. Kenny and Roy jogged up to it and looked in the passenger side window. The driver, a man of indeterminate age—he might have been anywhere from 30 to 50—gestured to the woman in the passenger seat to roll down her window. When she did, Kenny noticed she held a baby, an infant, close to her chest. "Where are you men headed?" the driver asked.

"Back to the Midwest," Roy said. "Wisconsin and Minnesota."

"You in the army?"

Kenny thought that was an odd question. They were still dressed in their uniforms, after all.

"Just discharged," Roy answered. "On our way home."

"Pile in the back," the man gestured with his thumb. "I can get you part of the way."

"Much obliged," Roy said. He opened the door for Kenny, who slid across the seat to the other side. Roy sat behind the woman.

"Name's Green," the driver told them, "Bob Green." Roy volunteered his and Kenny's names.

"That's Vanessa," Green said, nodding at the woman. She turned slightly and smiled at the two men in the back seat but didn't speak. She had black hair and dark skin, and Kenny thought she might be Mexican. She looked young, not much older than Roy or Kenny. The baby fussed a little, and she turned her attention back to it. Kenny couldn't tell if it was a boy or a girl.

"How'd you end up in Butte, of all places?" Green asked.

"Came out of Fort Lewis, Washington," Roy said. "Been hitchhiking to get back home."

"Finding rides okay?"

"Sure, people have been real nice. We must have had half a dozen different drivers pick us up so far."

Kenny counted them in his head. He came up with eight. "Coming up on the Continental Divide here, gentlemen," Green was saying. "This is Pipestone Pass. Elevation of over 6400 feet."

Snow once again lined the edges of the highway. Kenny had been driving the milk delivery truck back home for a few months before getting drafted and Jeeps in the army, mostly ferrying officers around. But he didn't think he'd want to drive through these mountains on a regular basis. Though, like anything else, he supposed, you'd get used to it.

"Continental Divide," Roy said. "I've heard of that. But I don't really know what it is, though."

"The Divide runs north-south along the Rocky Mountains," Green said. "Basically, it means that all the water on one side runs into the Pacific, and all the water on the other side flows out to the Atlantic."

"That's pretty simple. Guess I shoulda paid more attention in school," Roy joked.

Green chuckled.

The baby started to wail. "Shush, Mija," Vanessa said. She rocked the baby in her arms and the crying soon stopped.

"Damnedest thing," Green said. "Every time we go across the Divide, she starts to cry."

The baby—Kenny knew she was a girl now—was quiet again. Vanessa looked over at Green, then back at Kenny. She smiled and Kenny smiled back. Kenny wondered if they were married, if the baby was Green's daughter. Then again, Vanessa could have been his daughter and the baby his grandchild. Or maybe they weren't related at all. Green hadn't explained anything, and Kenny didn't ask.

They continued driving along highway 10. Kenny had seen more of the country than he'd ever imagined he would in the last several days. He remembered the sight of Mt.

Rainer National Park, and where the highway ran alongside the Walla Walla River, and the land around Missoula. Even the vistas while traveling through the mountains in Idaho were beautiful, if terrifying. But the area they traversed now—somehow this summed it all up. Snow-capped mountains rose in the distance to either side. Pine forests stretched out as far as he could see. They crossed mountain streams that gurgled and flowed rapidly. The air smelled fresh and clean. Kenny closed his eyes and breathed deeply.

"It's really pretty here," he heard Roy say. "Where exactly are we?"

"Just about smack in the middle of the state," Green said. "There's a turn-off up here that runs down to a little town called Bozeman. Just about the prettiest place you'd ever want to see. Unfortunately, we don't got time to go there. We're due in Billings this evening."

"Bozeman," Roy repeated. "I'm gonna remember that name." The baby began fussing again. Vanessa looked over at Green. Kenny thought she looked a little scared.

"She's just hungry," Vanessa said.

"Well, then feed her," Green said.

Vanessa looked back at Kenny and her lips twitched as though she wanted to smile but couldn't. Kenny smiled and nodded at her. She turned away, and he looked over at Roy, whose attention was focused out the side window.

"Livingston's up ahead, then Big Timber. We'll stop there for a few minutes. Rest. Stretch your legs if you want."

"That sounds fine," Kenny said, not knowing what else to say. Vanessa had turned toward the side window, and her back was to Kenny. She held the baby in front of her. Kenny heard a soft, sucking sound. He looked again at Roy, whose eyes went wide as he arched his eyebrows. A smile played about his lips and his eyes. Vanessa was breast feeding the baby.

Green pulled off the highway just outside of Big Timber. He shut off the ignition and turned to the men in the back seat. "Rest stop," he said. "Five minutes." He got out of the car.

Vanessa did too and walked a little ways away with Green. They talked in hushed tones, looking back at the car every now and then. Roy and Kenny stood near the back of the car and looked around. Kenny noticed that Green didn't touch Vanessa and didn't seem to pay much attention to the baby. He wished he had a cigarette, but he'd smoked his last one that morning in Missoula.

"What do you think of him?" Roy asked. "Green." Kenny looked back at the couple. Green had walked away from Vanessa. She stood, bouncing the baby in her arms, and talking to her. Kenny couldn't hear what she said and wondered if she was speaking Spanish. A couple of the soldiers back at base had known Spanish and used to speak to one another in it when they didn't want anyone else to know what they were saying. Some of the other soldiers didn't like that, and one night the two Spanish speakers had been roughed up a little, nothing too serious. They came away with some cuts and bruises but no broken bones. Kenny hadn't been a part of that, but the whole squadron had been punished when the C.O. heard about it. That had happened over a year ago, and Kenny had forgotten all about it until this moment.

"He's okay, I suppose," Kenny said.

"Do you believe that she took her tit out right there in the car?"

"To feed the baby."

"Did you get a look at it? Not the baby, I mean her tit?" Kenny didn't answer.

"I didn't," Roy said, disappointed.

Green walked back to the car followed at a short distance by Vanessa. "Saddle up," he said. "Time to get back on the road." The sun was just setting when the four of them arrived in Billings. "Not sure where you want to go," Green said, "but I gotta take Vanessa to the bus station. That might be as good a place as any to catch another ride."

"Sure," Roy said.

Outside the bus station, Green pulled a large suitcase from the trunk. Vanessa and the baby went inside. "Good luck, gentlemen," Green said.

"Thanks for the ride," Kenny said.

"Sure do appreciate it," Roy added.

Green turned without saying another word and followed Vanessa inside.

Kenny stretched. He couldn't believe how tired he felt. They'd been on the road for three days now. He looked around. There wasn't much to see here. He supposed if someone was dropping someone else off—or maybe picking someone up—they might get another ride. He figured they must be close to the Dakotas by now, but he wasn't sure.

Several men sat along the side of the building that housed the bus station. They were older men, grizzled, tough-looking. Kenny watched them warily. Each of them held a piece of wood and a knife. They were whittling, carving the wood. Kenny couldn't tell what kind of objects they were making. One of the men grunted each time he ran his knife down the length of the wood. He was unshaven and missing several teeth. He scowled when he noticed Kenny watching him.

Kenny looked away, down the other side of the street. It was quiet. No one else was out, and he didn't see any cars. Roy heaved a sigh. Kenny looked back at the whittlers. One of the other men had a long scar on his left cheek. He chewed tobacco and spit on the ground. A dark, wet spot grew near his feet. The last whittler looked older than the other two. He wore an old, stained fedora that was pushed back off his forehead. He looked at Kenny and Roy and grinned. He kept running his knife over the wood and leaned over to speak to the man next to him. Kenny was too far away to hear what was said, but the second man looked in their direction. He turned to the older man and shrugged.

Kenny turned to Roy. He looked tired and his uniform was rumpled from three days of travel. "I don't feel good about this," Kenny whispered. He indicated the three men whittling with a brief movement of his head. Roy looked past him at the men. He nodded.

"Maybe we should go inside," Roy said.

"The bus station?" Kenny asked.

"Yeah."

"Okay."

They walked inside. A half dozen or so people lounged on chairs and benches, waiting for their buses to arrive. Kenny didn't see Green or Vanessa or the baby anywhere.

"We met some good people," Roy said, "hitchhiking."

"Yeah," Kenny agreed. "We did." He thought about Bud, the Taubners, and Ranger Brook.

"But that road through the mountains in Idaho? I almost shit my pants."

Kenny looked at Roy, surprised. He hadn't known that Roy was as bothered by that part of the trip as he had been. "Maybe we should get tickets," Roy said. "The rest of the way home, I mean."

"We are at the bus station," Kenny said, grateful that Roy had made the suggestion.

"We probably saved some money getting this far," Roy said. He was trying to justify the decision. As far as Kenny was concerned, he didn't need to. Kenny liked the idea of a comfortable bus ride the rest of the way home.

Down a hallway with a sign marked "Rest Rooms," a door opened, and out came Vanessa carrying the baby on one arm and a suitcase in the opposite hand. She walked over to a bench and sat down without looking at Kenny and Roy. She held the baby on her lap and bounced her gently on one knee.

"I'll see how much tickets cost," Roy said. He walked over to the ticket counter. Kenny watched Vanessa and the baby for a moment, then he turned and followed Roy.

2. "Beatles '75"

M y favorite album—ever—is "Beatles '75". I'm sure that's true for a lot of people. Anyway, that's where it all started." I nodded and leaned back in my chair, listening. My mini recorder sat on the table between us. Dr. Austen wore a buttoned-down blue shirt, a striped, red tie loose around his neck, and wire rimmed glasses. His light brown hair was trimmed short and neat. He didn't look like a mad scientist.

"Many scientists—theorists like me, in particular—maintain some kind of hobby outside the profession. It helps us to cope, to think."

"How do you mean?"

"To cope or to think? Both, I suppose. Well, the work can be incredibly stressful sometimes. You might not think so, as we're off in our labs, our sterile, protected environments, removed from the normal quotidian reality that most people live in. But that's just it; we need something to connect us to the rest of the world, to anchor us, if you will. And those hobbies, in turn, can invigorate us in our work. Outside activities help stimulate the thought process, streams of consciousness, different neural pathways. Science has confirmed all this, of course."

"Of course."

"My particular hobby—my obsession, some would contend—is music."

"The mathematics of it?" I suggested.

"The beauty of it." He looked past me, off into the distance, lost in thought. Or memory.

A moment passed. I cleared my throat.

He returned to the present, the here and now. "Piano lessons as a child. I learned guitar in high school, played in a couple different bands. Nothing that ever went anywhere.

Switched to bass when I started college, my undergraduate years. That's what I've been focused on since."

He paused and stared at me. I didn't know if he'd lost his train of thought or forgot what we'd been talking about.

"So," I prodded him, ""Beatles '75"."

"What have you heard about the Alternative Worlds Project?" I was taken aback by the abrupt change of subject.

"Just what I read on the 'net," I said.

"Rumors and innuendo. Disinformation." I didn't know where he was going with this, but his eyes seemed to light up. A smile played about his lips. He continued, "As a journalist—well-read, informed—have you been able to dig through the layers of speculation, of outright lies, to find a kernel of truth underneath?"

This was getting weird. "I'm a music journalist," I protested. Austen chuckled and shook his head.

"Now you are. But I know your history, Mr. Kent. I've done my homework. It's the reason I specifically requested you for this interview."

"I didn't know you had," I said. All I did know was that I was here to interview Dr. Herman Austen, who supposedly possessed some new information on the recording of "Beatles '75", one of the most famous and influential records in music history. What he might know or where he'd gained such knowledge, I had no idea. In fact, I was skeptical that he knew anything new at all. "Beatles '75" had been reviewed, discussed, dissected, and argued over for the last twenty-five years.

"The Alternative Worlds Project, Mr. Kent? What do you know—or believe you know—about it?"

I didn't understand where Austen was going with this, or why, but I decided to play along for the moment.

"Some kind of super-secret, hush-hush government project, supposedly trying to prove the existence of alternate dimensions or some such. If it even exists."

Austen smiled, but he did not look pleased.

"Other universes—'alternate dimensions,' as you so quaintly put it—were discovered—and 'proven'—quite some time ago. Although that information has not been shared with the general public. Hush-hush, as you say."

"Are you connected to the Alternative Worlds Project in some way?"

"I wouldn't say it's been my life's work, Mr. Kent, but I have been a part of the Project for many years."

"And the doctor in your title is for ...?"

"Theoretical physics. String theory. Quantum mechanics. Plus a few other esoteric fields that you probably don't have a name for yet, much less an understanding of."

"Theoretical physics?"

Austen nodded. "Although the division between theory and practical applications has become . . . fuzzy, of late."

"Okay, hold up a minute. You're telling me that the Alternative Worlds Project is a real thing? And you work on it?"

"That's exactly what I'm telling you, Mr. Kent."

I didn't know whether to believe him—I was leaning toward not—but decided to follow up for now. "And these alternate dimensions were discovered some time ago?"

"Years, in fact."

"So why does the Project still exist? If it's already accomplished its goals?"

"Goals change, Mr. Kent. They evolve. Once we proved the existence of other universes, the next step should be obvious. Contact. The chance to travel between universes."

"Okay. Even if I believe you—and let me tell you, that's a huge leap of faith—why are you telling me of all people?"

""Beatles '75"."

He left that hang in the air like it was the most obvious answer in the world, as though it answered all my questions instead of raising a dozen more.

"I'm sorry," I said. "I'm not following you."

"Like I said, it's my favorite record of all time—by anyone, not just the Beatles. It's just sublime. I can't say enough about it. From the opening song, *This Guitar Can't Keep from Crying*. You know, the sheer surprise of starting with one of George's songs. The only other time they'd done that was on "Revolver." All the way through, it's hard to pick out a favorite song. Everything flows together so well. I know a lot of people would say *Whatever Gets You Through the Night*, John and Paul harmonizing on vocals. Or Paul's *Venus and Mars* suite that takes up most of side two on the original LP version. That's a real highlight for me. And the closer—another Harrison song, *Can't Stop Thinking About You*. That's one of the greatest love songs ever written for my money. It's amazing."

Austen spoke faster as he went on. He was enthused. His love for "Beatles '75" clearly showed. "It's a great album," I said. "Lots of people love it."

"I'm sorry. I know I can go on interminably about it. I've studied every song on the record, their nuances, their changes, the lyrics, the subtext, everything."

"Okay, but what does this have to do with the Alternative Worlds Project?"

Austen took a deep breath before answering. "Once we'd proved the existence of other universes, not just in theory, mind you, but through direct observation—and don't bother asking. The mechanics are arduous enough and the science behind it is probably understood by no more than a handful of people on the entire planet. Fortunately, most of us worked on the Project. We spent years developing and refining the technology. The Window—that was the nickname we gave to our Observation Portal—was simplicity itself, a child's toy compared to where we headed next. We first called it The Door."

"A door into another universe?"

"It's not as easy as it sounds."

I wondered if that was a joke. Looking at Dr. Austen, I could see it wasn't.

He continued, "The Door eventually morphed into a more complex technology. We call it The Bridge."

"The Bridge?"

"The Bridge allowed travel to other universes—where we could observe, interact, and then return to our original world. That was the theory anyway. In practice, it proved a bit more . . . problematic. Months were spent in discussion on how to proceed—or even if we should proceed. We could travel to other worlds, but some argued that didn't mean we should. They missed the whole point of science."

"So you found you could travel to another universe—or universes?"

"Early string theory pointed toward ten or eleven dimensions. Most people can only comprehend the four that we can observe and that appear to relate to our normal, everyday lives. Without going into technical specifics, string theory led to our concept of the multiverse, many universes existing simultaneously. That's as simple as I can make it. No offense."

"None taken. If I understand the theory, these other universes exist alongside ours but are different in some way. In one, I might have worn a green shirt today instead of this blue one. In another, I might be a lawyer instead of a journalist."

Austen did smile then. "Very good, Mr. Kent. You're proving me right—that I was correct in asking for you specifically. That's a simplistic way of looking at a very complex issue, but you're essentially correct. Without some grounding in theoretical physics, I'm afraid I can't really simplify it enough to explain it to you. Suffice it to say that studying the higher dimensions of string theory allowed us to make a leap - the question arises: if the multiverse exists—which we knew it did—how many other universes are out there? Can you imagine?"

I shook my head. I couldn't.

"It's infinite. As far as we can determine, there's no end to the multiverse. Infinite space in our universe is a concept that most non-scientists accept but can't comprehend. The physical universe just extends and extends—there's no end to it. The multiverse expands that concept in another direction if you will."

Austen paused. I felt he was waiting for me to catch up. Other dimensions, an infinite number of them, and they'd developed a way to travel there. Austen was right; I might be able to accept it, but comprehension was a whole other thing.

After a moment, he continued, "Anyway, the next question became: if we traveled to another universe, could we bring something back to our own as proof that it existed, that we'd actually ventured to another world? We are scientists, after all; we require proof, preferably physical proof. Al-Hasan and I—that's Dr. Al-Hasan, the Egyptian physicist? You've never heard of him? No. Regardless, Al-Hasan and I were tasked with deciding what we might use as proof. We wanted something small, something compact," he chuckled, "something that could be easily transported."

Austen paused and took a deep breath. He reached down to the bag he'd brought with him and withdrew a small object. With an aura of great solemnity, he placed it on the table between us. It was a compact disc in a jewel case.

"Beatles '75".

"You're quite familiar with the album, I assume," he said.

"Sure," I said. I picked it up and flipped it over, scanning the song titles listed on the back. I had my own copy at home, of course, and this one looked identical to that. Until—"Wait a minute—where's *Goodnight Vienna?*"

"Indeed. Tell me about *Goodnight Vienna.*"

I looked up at Austen blankly. Once again, I didn't know where this was headed. "It's Ringo's song," I said. "Well, John wrote it, but Ringo sings lead. It's his one lead vocal on the album."

"Exactly right. In our world."

I scanned the song list on the CD. "*Since My Baby Left Me?* What's this?"

"An old R & B song from the '50s. John sings it."

"Wait, what do you mean, 'in our world'? Are you telling me this CD …?"

"Is from another universe, yes."

I set the CD down on the table as though it might burn me, but I couldn't take my eyes off it. *Goodbye, Vienna* should have been the third track on the disc, but *Since My Baby Left Me* took its place there.

"It's perfectly safe to handle, Mr. Kent."

"You've listened to this?"

"Yes, of course."

"And you're telling me it's not some kind of alternate version, released in the U.K. or Eastern Europe or somewhere?"

"Have you ever heard of such a release, Mr. Kent?" I had to admit I hadn't.

"Where did you get this? I mean, how did you find it? I mean—I'm not sure what to ask you."

"Take a breath, Mr. Kent. Consider the reason I asked specifically for you for this interview. I've followed your career. For some time, I've been quite an aficionado of your music related journalism. And I did some research into you. You have a background in science."

"I just wrote a few articles," I protested.

"Don't be humble, Mr. Kent. Your writing was well researched, well documented. I know those who were sorry to see you switch career tracks, though as I said, I've enjoyed your writing about music as well. In any case, you've made an impression, Mr. Kent."

"What about ...?" I nudged the CD with one finger.

"We believed the Bridge would allow us to travel to an infinite number of other worlds, other universes. The question arose: how would we decide where to visit, and how could we control that destination? The Bridge utilizes the user's brain patterns and brain waves. I realize that probably sounds metaphysical and unscientific, but believe me, it's not. By using quantum mechanics in conjunction with the user's brain wave activity; utilizing a computer system decades beyond anything that existed elsewhere in the world—all developed by those of us in the Project, you understand—well, Al-Hasan and I theorized the user could essentially determine his own destination. Whatever one thought about—whatever was foremost in your mind—would draw you to a world where that subject maintained a certain degree of importance. Or, as we soon discovered, a world where that subject offered a difference—a change—from our world. Of course, this is all in layman's terms, you know."

"Of course."

"I am attempting not to overwhelm you. It's difficult."

"You went to another universe where there's a Beatles album with a different song on it?"

"It's slightly more complicated than that. The reason *Goodbye Vienna* doesn't appear on this album is that, in the universe this CD comes from, Ringo Starr was no longer a member of the Beatles in 1975."

"What?" I grabbed the CD, opened the jewel case, and pulled out the booklet inside.

"When I entered the Bridge, my primary thoughts were about music, specifically the Beatles and my favorite album."

""Beatles '75","" I said, as I slowly opened the CD booklet to the centerfold.

""Beatles '75","" Dr. Austen echoed. "When I arrived in the other universe, everything seemed the same. I wasn't sure that I had actually crossed over. Landmarks were the same, buildings were identical. People on the street appeared no different from those I saw every day. I wandered about a bit until I found a record store, one I recognized in the same place on the same street as our world. One I'd been to before. I went in, found this CD, and purchased it."

Apparently, our money worked in this other world, but that was a fleeting thought. My hands shook as I opened the CD booklet. I expected to see the famous photograph of all four Beatles, smiling and joking with one another, caught in what seemed to be an unguarded moment. I loved that image. What I saw stunned me. Paul, John, and George, looking much the same—they wore the same outfits, although their poses were altered. The three of them laughed and looked happy. But there was no Ringo.

"How...?" I began, but I wasn't sure where that sentence was going.

"You remember the tensions within the band in '68 and '69?"

"Of course." Everyone knew about that.

"Well, in the world I found myself in, Ringo either quit or was fired from the group after "The White Album." The clerk I spoke with was unsure of what actually happened— and surprised by my questions. I think she thought I was quite mad."

"And the other three just went on without him?" I flipped to the back of the CD booklet where the credits were printed.

"And apparently to just as great a success. Which, perhaps, says something about Ringo I'm not sure I'm willing to consider."

"Jim Keltner?" I read off the credits.

"A session drummer—" Austen began.

"I know who Jim Keltner is. He's the drummer on this album?"

"Apparently they used a series of session drummers over the years."

"No permanent replacement for Ringo? No fifth Beatle?"

"Not in this world, no."

I slipped the CD booklet back into the jewel case and flipped it over. The rest of the songs—besides *Since My Baby Left Me*—were familiar to me.

"You've listened to this?" I repeated. "All of it?"

"Multiple times."

"And the music? It's the same as—as the version …?"

"A few subtle differences exist. Of course, the drumming is an obvious one. Any Beatles fan or scholar would pick up on that right away. A slightly longer guitar solo here and there, a more prominent piano on *Can't Stop Thinking About You*. But for the most part, it's the same music we've heard before. I didn't find a single change in the lyrics."

"This is amazing. There's never been anything like this in the history of rock music."

"Or in the entire history of our universe, to be frank. Al-Hasan and I wanted something that would prove our discovery beyond a doubt, but something that the common man could readily understand. I knew when I found this CD, it was the right choice. It proved I'd been to another universe." He paused, then gestured at the CD. "That was the first one."

"The first one?"

Dr. Austen stared silently at me for a few seconds that seemed to take an eternity to pass. Then he reached down into his bag and pulled out another CD and handed it to me. I recognized it. The cover of "Beatles '75" had become iconic, a simple tan background with the title printed in large black letters, just slightly off center. It was a variation on what we commonly called "The White Album."

I looked up from the disc in my hand at Austen. He said nothing but nodded almost imperceptibly. I slowly turned the disc over and looked at the back cover in astonishment.

"What is this?" I asked.

"Another universe, another variation."

Many of the songs I knew from "Beatles '75"—our world's version of "Beatles '75"—were present, but the running order was radically shifted around. The album opened with *Whatever Gets You Through the Night* instead of *This Guitar Can't Keep from Crying,* followed by *Venus and Mars* and *Listen to What the Man Said,* though a couple of the other songs that made up the *Venus and Mars Suite,* a series of songs written by Paul, were missing. Most notably, both of George's contributions to the album were gone (although *Goodbye Vienna* was back). Smack in the middle of the track listing—I read the title aloud—*The Sky Is Crying*—then looked up at Austen. "The Stevie Ray Vaughan song?"

He nodded. "Written in 1959 by Elmore James."

"King of the slide guitar."

Austen smiled. "You know your music history, Mr. Kent. Elmore James was a favorite of both George and John."

"'Elmore James got nothin' on this, baby,'" I quoted George's line from "Let It Be" when he responds to John's slide guitar solo. "This replaces George's original songs? I'm surprised to see the Beatles doing cover songs at this stage of their career."

"You noticed the last song on the album?"

I had. I slid the CD booklet out of the jewel case. I opened it to the centerfold. There he stood, alongside Paul, John, and Ringo. "Eric Clapton," I said. "There were rumors that John wanted him to replace George around the time of "Let It Be.'"

"George walked out on the Beatles for several days in January of '69."

"But he came back," I protested, then paused. "And you found a universe where he didn't."

Austen nodded.

"But Clapton and Harrison were close. Even after Clapton married George's ex-wife, Pattie, they remained good friends. I can't believe he'd take George's place in the group."

"I stayed a bit longer in this universe than the first," Austen said. "After my disappointing conversation with the record store clerk about Ringo—well, I made it a point to do a bit more research on my own before returning home. In the world where I obtained this disc, history played a bit differently. George walked out on the band during the rehearsals for "Let It Be," same as he did in our world. However, when John suggested replacing him with Eric Clapton, the others went along with the idea. When George heard about it, he rang up Eric himself and encouraged him to join the group. Clapton's joining The Beatles energized Paul and John, both of whom had wanted to 'get back' to the simpler aspects of being a live band after their years in the studio. "Let It Be" was released under its original title "Get Back," and marked the debut of Clapton replacing George in the band."

"And after that?"

"They continued on with Clapton as an official member, contributing a few songs to each album, just as George had done—"

"Or was allowed to do."

"Or was allowed to do," Austen conceded. "And eventually, we get to "Beatles '75"."

I lifted the CD off the table. "And the music on this one?"

"A lot more substantial changes than the first one I showed you. Having Clapton in the band seems to have affected both John's and Paul's approach to music and songwriting. The same songs, for the most part, but maybe best described as being a bit more raw. If that makes sense."

It did. "And the last song here?" I asked.

"Clapton's well-known cover of Bob Marley's *I Shot the Sheriff*. Only here, he and John share lead vocals, with Paul and Ringo playing the reggae beat. You've got to hear it to believe it."

That much was true, certainly, but I wondered if I'd ever actually get to hear the music on these discs. What did Austen intend to do with them? Why had he chosen me to be the one to tell all this to?

"It sounds like you prefer this version of "Beatles '75"," I said.

"Prefer? No, not in the least. I find the alterations, the differences extremely interesting. As a scientist. From the viewpoint of a music fan, they can't quite compare with the original. Or what's original to us, anyway."

"I take it you prefer George in the group. And Ringo?"

"Of course. Unlike some people, I've never been able to pick a favorite Beatle. Depending on the day or my mood, it could well be any of the four."

I turned the disc over in my hand, thinking about what Austen had just said. "On the world where you found this," I mused, "Eric Clapton is probably someone's favorite Beatle. They probably think the band wasn't as good until he came along."

"I have considered that, Mr. Kent, and no doubt you are right. As inconceivable as that may be to you or me. No, I much prefer our world's version of The Beatles to any I've discovered elsewhere. And I think you'll see why." He reached down into his bag and pulled out two more jewel boxes. "The changes on those first two discs are minor compared to what you're about to see."

I knew where this was going, but Austen paused for a moment, looking at the two discs in his hand, as though he couldn't decide which one to show me first. The cover of the one he handed me looked slightly different than what I was used to. It had the same tan background, the title just off center, but something—and I couldn't put my finger on precisely what—seemed off. Maybe the font was different. I turned it over to read the song titles. When Austen spoke, quieter now, his voice quavered just a little.

"You've seen versions of The Beatles without Ringo or George but imagine what they'd be without John."

"*This Guitar Can't Keep from Crying* was once again the opening track, but the titles after that were jumbled. *Venus and Mars* was followed by *Rock Show,* then *I Shot the Sheriff* appeared as it had on the previous disc Austen had shown me. Next was *Call Me*, a song I didn't recognize.

"Written and sung by Ringo," Austen replied in answer to my question. "A throwaway, in my opinion."

"*Sprits of Ancient Egypt*," I read. That song was part of Paul's *Venus and Mars Suite*, but here it stood on its own, probably as the first song on side two of the LP version, I guessed, from its placement. "I love that song. But it looks out of place here."

"Tell me what you like about it."

"The heavy, crunchy guitar sound. The interplay between John's and George's guitars. The yearning in Paul's voice. One of his best vocal takes, I think."

"I totally agree. But this version has several changes. The guitars sound similar—without John, of course—but the lead vocal's been given to Eric Clapton."

"Clapton again."

"Yes, taking John's place this time."

That would account for the presence of *I Shot the Sheriff,* but I wondered how they'd got to this point in this universe. "What happened?" I asked.

"Sometime in 1970—as near as I can tell; both "Let It Be" and "Abbey Road" appeared to be the same as our universe's versions—John quit the band to strike out on his own with Yoko. The other three Beatles decided to continue on without him and brought Clapton into the group."

"That makes more sense to me than the last one, I guess, Clapton and George being such good mates and all. But without John, how could they still be like the Beatles?"

"Not so much like we know them."

I looked at the disc. The next song was *Call Me Back Again*, another one I had never heard of. I said as much to Austen. "It's a McCartney song," Austen shook his head. "Not Lennon-McCartney, you understand."

"But the two of them were writing their own songs anyway, almost exclusively by '75. There wasn't much collaboration in the writing process."

"True enough. But there was a lot in the studio, especially in the early '70s, after they each kind of did their own thing in the late '60s. And the songs still always bore the Lennon-McCartney credit."

I shrugged. People had been discussing Paul and John's collaborations against their individual creations *ad nauseam* for a long time. "It seems weird to have a song called *Call Me Back Again* on the same album as one titled *Call Me*. Is this one a response to Ringo's song in some way?"

"I don't know. The two songs don't seem to be related in any way, other than the similarity in the titles."

Call Me Back Again was followed by a couple more McCartney songs. I knew them although neither had been on "Beatles '75". (*Jet* had appeared on an earlier Beatles album, and the silly *Magneto and Titanium Man* had only shown up as a B-side on one the album's singles.) The final song on the disc should have been *Can't Stop Thinking About You* since George was still a member of this world's Beatles, but it wasn't.

"*Not Guilty?*" I read.

"Another song of George's."

"There were rumors of an outtake with this title from "The White Album"."

"I'm impressed, Mr. Kent. That's not exactly common knowledge."

I smiled at the compliment. "Supposedly nothing more than a demo ever existed."

"Yes, that's my understanding as well, an early take that was never developed. But this is a full band version. George plays acoustic guitar, Clapton electric."

"Why the change? What happened to *Can't Stop Thinking About You?*"

"Who knows? Maybe John pushed for *Can't Stop Thinking*. Maybe Clapton liked *Not Guilty* more and thought it worthy of being resurrected. There's really no way to answer that question; it's just pure speculation at this point."

Maybe Clapton did know the song. He had played lead guitar on George's *While My Guitar Gently Weeps* on "The White Album" after all. Maybe he'd been there when George demoed it for the others back in '68. Maybe George had played it for him in the intervening years. Austen was right: nothing but pointless speculation.

"Every alternate version of "Beatles '75" you've shown me is a greater departure than the one before. And that disc you're holding—even more so, I'm guessing?"

"I'm afraid that's right, Mr. Kent. But before I show you this, I need to backtrack for a moment. I want to make something perfectly clear to you. As I told you at the beginning of our conversation, "Beatles '75" is my all-time favorite album, and it served as the anchor point for my journeys through the Bridge—to other universes. I've listened to the Beatles my whole life. I've read about them, studied them, learned how to play the music—I'm a consummate fan, if you will."

"I get it. Many people think of them as the greatest band of all time."

"Absolutely. I'm one of those people. And that's the important point: they were a band. Not just four lads who played together. A band. Each contributed an essential part in what made them what they were, what made them The Beatles. I don't consider any one of them more important than the others in making them what they were—what they are to us in our world."

"Even Ringo?" I joked.

"Even Ringo," Austen replied seriously. "That's why I find these alternate universe versions so fascinating and so disappointing at the same time. But this—" he paused, looking at the disc in his hands.

"That's the Beatles—"Beatles '75"—without Paul?"

"Yes," Austen sighed and handed the disc to me.

I was shocked. Even at first glance, this looked nothing like the other versions. The plain tan background was gone. Here, five faces looked out from the cover, photographs that appeared to be retouched and re-colored. The album title—still "Beatles '75," I noted with some degree of relief—ran across the top in bold lettering. John's picture, with shorter hair than I was used to in '75, but the same trademark round granny glasses, sat in the center. John smiled like a man who knew something the photographer didn't. The upper right corner showed George caught mid-laugh, and the lower right a bearded, serious Ringo. The picture in the lower left corner was Yoko Ono, looking demure and downcast. The upper left-hand corner showed a bearded man I didn't recognize. It wasn't Clapton.

"No Clapton this time?" I asked.

Austen shook his head. He'd become more serious, even dour. "With Paul out of the picture, and Yoko elevated to an official member—at least by '75—I imagine what the others felt they needed most was a bass player. Paul's an amazing musician; as you know, he can—and does—play everything. And the whole world knows his voice and his songs. But his bass playing sometimes gets overlooked. He's one of the best."

"And this is …?" I held up the disc.

"Klaus Voorman."

I knew the name, mostly for his session work. And he'd designed and drawn the artwork for the "Revolver" album cover. He had been a good friend of the band, and apparently in some other world, a literal fifth Beatle. I turned the disc over. The back cover was plain white with song titles printed in black. Most of them I didn't know. I looked up at Austen, confused.

"Ask any questions you want," he said. "I've listened to it enough times; I should be able to answer anything you want to know."

I had plenty of questions. I decided to start at the top, with the first song. "*I'm the Greatest?*"

"Written by John, sung by Ringo. A bit of a tongue-in-cheek take, emphasized by Ringo's vocal, on the band's own popularity. It's Ringo's one lead vocal on the album. I find it odd that it's the lead off track."

Goodbye, Vienna—the John-penned song sung by Ringo on my world's version of the album—wasn't listed, missing in this universe. *Instant Karma* came next. I recognized it as one of John's songs, but it had been released several years earlier as a single only, later collected on several Beatles compilations. George's *This Guitar Can't Keep from Crying* was third, demoted from its usual place as the first song on the album. After that, things got weird.

"What the heck is *Bring on the Lucie*?" I asked.

"Another Lennon original. I suppose it could loosely be described as a protest song. Backing vocals by Yoko."

"And the next song, *World of Stone*? Another one of John's, I suppose?"

"No, that's actually by George. It's a nice melody; John plays piano on it. It's one of George's more spiritual songs—that side of him comes out more strongly here than we're used to."

"Maybe Paul kept that side in check, with his pop sensibilities."

"Perhaps. With Paul being gone, George contributed more songs to this version of "Beatles '75"."

"I can see that," I said. *"Can't Stop Thinking About You* came up later in the track listing. With that, *This Guitar* and this *World of Stone* that made three."

"Four," Austen corrected me. *"Ooh Baby (You Know That I Love You)* is the other George song."

"Really? That title doesn't sound like Harrison."

"Maybe not the George we know in our universe. It's a very soulful song, almost like something out of 1960s' Motown." I raised my eyebrows at that. "Really," Austen added.

I looked back at the disc. *No Bed for John* was the final song from side one. The CD version here clearly separated the two sides of the original LP.

"That is a song by Yoko Ono," Austen told me. "Certainly nothing you or I would ever have expected to hear on a Beatles record."

I nodded and let it pass. I wasn't sure I wanted to know more about that. The song that would have been first on side two of the vinyl was listed as *Whatever Gets Us Through the Night.*

"'Us'?" I asked.

"Yes, it's the same song we know so well, only with slightly revised lyrics. I don't know why."

"Maybe Yoko's more prominent presence?"

"Maybe," Austen assented.

"*Can't Stop Thinking About You* was next, then *Since My Baby Left Me*, the song I'd seen on the Ringo-less version of "Beatles '75" that started this whole thing.

"John must have really liked that song," Austen said when I mentioned it. "That one and the next song"—I looked down at the disc; *Nobody Knows You When You're Down and Out* followed—"are both cover songs, both sung by John."

"That's an old blues number."

"Yes. Ironically, in our world, probably Eric Clapton recorded the best-known version."

"Who's not a part of this world's version of the Beatles." Austen moved his head in a kind of combination shake and nod.

The next song was George's *Ooh Baby*. That was followed by one I'd never heard of. I read the title aloud, "*Mum's Only Looking for Her Hand in the Snow?*"

"Another song by Yoko. The music is kind of bluesy, or blues based. John plays lead guitar, George contributes a slide solo. But the vocals ..."

"Bad?"

"Screechy."

I understood what Austen meant. John had produced a couple of albums by his wife Yoko, but they were critical and commercial failures and quickly faded into obscurity. I'd heard one of them, and although most of it was difficult to listen to, there were definite hints of decent songs hidden within.

I set the CD back on the table between us. "So," I said, "I guess this is the end of your story. Each alternate version of "Beatles '75" you've shown me has gone further from the original. Each universe had a different Beatle leave the band."

"Yes, although I caution you on your use of the 'original.' When you delve into the theory—or the fact, I should say—of multiple universes, you realize that our world is just one in a spectrum—an infinite spectrum—of worlds. Discussing the originality of one universe over another is problematic at best."

"But that would mean …" I stopped. I had no idea what that meant.

"No matter. We can talk about our universe as the original, as it is original to us. A matter of semantics, I suppose, but it makes the discussion easier."

"Okay, the further you traveled from our world by means of this Bridge of yours, the worse things got? I mean, in terms of the music."

"In a way, that's true. However, remember that I said, and my belief remains, that The Beatles were greater than just a sum of their parts. I don't believe one is more important than the others."

"But given these four discs you've collected, one could easily make the claim that Paul—and John, to a lesser extent—was more important to the band than Ringo, or even George."

"It depends on how you choose to define 'importance,' Mr. Kent. As the main songwriters, they definitely had more of an effect on the direction of the band. But all of these versions show significant changes. If you listen to that first disc I showed you, you will see, or rather hear, that the Beatles without Ringo are simply not The Beatles of our world."

"What should I take away from all this then? What's your point?"

"My point, Mr. Kent," he began, then paused. "I collected these discs to prove the existence of other worlds, to prove that we'd developed the technology to travel to them, that we had traveled there. But I began to realize that my fellow scientists, who didn't share my love for music, for this music in particular, didn't quite see the significance of the difference in the other worlds in the same way that I did."

"I see," I said, though I wasn't so sure I did.

"I haven't quite reached the apex of my story, Mr. Kent. I recently traveled via the Bridge to one more world."

"You have another CD?" What could this one be? I'd already seen discs from four different worlds where each of the Beatles had left the band before 1975.

"I don't have another disc to show you. I didn't bring back any evidence from the fifth world I visited. A visit that left me feeling . . . what I can only describe as despair."

"What happened?"

Austen was reluctant to continue, but after a moment, he spoke again. This was what he'd brought me here to tell me, after all, but I could tell he found it difficult to say. "On this world, there was no "Beatles '75"."

I felt stunned, like I'd been punched in the head. "They never recorded it?"

Austen simply shook his head no.

"Why?" I managed to sputter out.

"On this world, "Beatles '75" didn't exist because the Beatles broke up in 1970."

"What?"

"After "Abbey Road" and "Let It Be," the same versions we know, the band broke up. The four of them went their separate ways."

Now I was truly stunned. "But The Beatles recorded dozens of records after 1970. "Beatles '75" might be your favorite, but what about…?" I wanted to name some of their records from the '80s and '90s. I had copies of all them at home, but the look in Austen's eyes made me stop.

"On that world, there are no Beatles records after "Let It Be." The Beatles, as a band, ceased to be in 1970."

Dr. Austen slumped in his chair. I tried to wrap my head around everything I'd been told. Before today, the concept of alternate worlds was just a theory, something out of science fiction movies or comic books. Now I had four CDs sitting in front of me, proof that such worlds existed, but proof that made them seem dismal places compared with the real world, my world. If Austen let me, I knew I'd take these CDs home and listen to them eventually. But tonight, I'd stay up all night, listening to my other Beatles records, the newer ones. And the thought of a world where The Beatles had existed as a band for only a decade, maybe even a bit less?

I looked across the table at Austen, understood and shared in his despair, as a single tear rolled slowly down his cheek.

3. Laura

Author's note: I have revised and rewritten Laura many times over the years since its first draft. In the last revision, I chose to set the story in the town of Minnisapa, the town created by my friend Kevin Fenton for his novel Merit Badges. The plot of the story and the main characters (Brian Gilmore, Laura Anderson, & Becky Pulaski) are all mine. The setting of Minnisapa and the other secondary characters in Laura were created by and are used with the kind permission of Kevin Fenton.

T he fall breeze chilled me, so I stuck my hands into the pockets of my jean jacket to keep them warm. The wind stirred my hair and it brushed against the back of my neck; it had grown long over the summer. Despite the chilly day, I felt comfortable.

I sat on the grass along the eastern edge of Lake Minnisapa, between the water and the paved bike-slash-walking path that circled it. A small park with picnic tables, swings, and other play equipment lay on the other side of the path, though the park was empty at the moment. Maybe it was too cold for little kids to be outside playing. A bunch of ducks bobbed in the water near the shore, staying well clear of the areas where a light film of algae and scum covered the surface. Every now and then one of them would duck its head under water, searching for food. Without warning, and almost like they had a pre-arranged signal, the flock lifted from the water, flew partway across the lake, and landed on the southern shore, next to the highway, maybe three-fourths of a mile from where I sat.

The sharp squeal of bicycle brakes and high-pitched voices caused me to turn my head. Two girls had stopped on the path. "Laura!" one of them yelled at the other. "I almost hit you." Laura Anderson, slightly shorter than her friend Becky Pulaski, had long, blond hair and a fresh round face red from the chill. My attention was focused more on her than her friend.

Laura waved at me and yelled, "Hey, Brian." She wore brightly colored, striped mittens, though she was out bike riding. I smiled at that. Becky glared at Laura. Their bikes weren't really that close to one another, though I surmised that Becky had had to brake rather abruptly. My own bike— an old brown Schwinn I'd had for years—lay in the grass between the path and where I sat.

"Hi, Laura," I shouted back, maybe just a bit too loud. A bit quieter, I added, "Hi, Becky."

Laura dismounted, parking her bike just off the path, and walked over to me. I figured that the polite, gentlemanly thing to do would be to stand, but by the time that thought had made it into my head, Laura had already lowered herself to the ground next to me. I hadn't graduated top of my class or anything, but I considered myself a pretty smart guy. I earned As and Bs in high school, except for tenth grade biology, the one low point on my GPA. Somehow when I was around Laura, my thought processes moved at a considerably slower rate.

"I haven't seen you around much," Laura said.

"Yeah, it's been a while," I said. *Through no fault of my own,* I thought. *I wanted to see you, tried to see you, longed to see you.*

"Laura," Becky whined. She was still on the path, straddling her bike, one foot resting on a pedal. "Let's go."

"C'mon, Becky, we need a break," Laura said, turning and looking back at her friend. Her face was very close to mine when she turned her head, her voice loud in my ear. I didn't mind. "Come sit down." Becky sighed but swung one leg over the bike. Laura looked at me; I was lost in those brown eyes. "We've been riding around the lake," she added conspiratorially.

"Oh," I said. Oh? That was it? What a conversationalist. The same thing happened every time I was near her.

Becky sat down on Laura's other side without speaking to either of us. She looked out over the lake, her face frozen into a mask of annoyance. I knew that Becky didn't really like me, though I didn't know why. We'd never had much contact back in school. Maybe I was wrong. I'd never been good at reading others, especially girls. But she was pissed off now, that was sure.

The three of us sat there in silence for a while. The breeze had died down for the moment and the sun shone warmly on my face. I should have been content. Think of something to say, I urged myself.

"Do you leave for school soon?" Laura asked, breaking the silence. I could have kissed her for that, and for about a hundred other reasons.

"About three weeks yet," I answered. "We start real late." I was going away, to Minneapolis, to the big city, for college. Three weeks is a long time, long enough to start something, I thought. Of course, three years of high school hadn't been long enough. I'd known Laura since our speech class together in tenth grade.

"We just finished our third—no, our second week," Laura said, looking over at Becky for confirmation. Becky nodded without looking at us. Laura was at Minnisapa State. "Are you scared to be going away from home?"

What kind of a question was that? My friends, the guys, and I never talked openly about stuff like that. I couldn't imagine Chimes asking that question.

"Not really," I answered. "I haven't really thought about it, I guess." She brushed away a few strands of hair that the wind had blown across her face. I smiled, again noticing the mittens she wore. Girls could get away with stuff like that. She looked cute. Then again, "cute" didn't seem exactly the right word to describe Laura.

Becky stood up. "I have to get home," she said.

"Okay," Laura said, smiling, not really looking up at Becky. "I'm going to stay here and talk to Brian for a while, okay?"

"Sure." Becky didn't sound at all happy.

"Call me tomorrow," Laura yelled as Becky rode off. Then she whispered, "She's mad at me."

"Why?"

"I don't know." She thought for a moment. "She doesn't like college very much. I think the pressure's getting to her." I nodded. I hadn't started school yet, but I wondered how much pressure there could be in the first two weeks. I guessed I'd find out. "I'm glad I saw you sitting here," Laura said. "It gave me an excuse to get away from Becky."

That's all I am to you. An excuse. I wanted to be more, so much more, but I had no idea how to make that happen. "Well, I mean," Laura stammered, "it's nice to see you anyway. I mean . . . you know," she finished. I'd never seen her nervous before, certainly not around me.

"Of course." I smiled. *What do you do*, I wondered, *read my thoughts? If you can, why don't you ever read the right ones?* I had longed for Laura since the first time I saw her. In our tenth-grade speech class, she'd used the word "sword," pronouncing it with the "w." When some of us corrected her, telling her the "w" was silent, she insisted that it was correct either way. For the rest of our sophomore year, whenever we passed each other in the hall, I'd say "sword," with the correct pronunciation, and she'd say "sword" pronouncing the "w." It was our special thing, but never went beyond that. I tried to sit next to her whenever we had a class together. I spent plenty of time staring at her across the library or during lunch in the concourse. But that was it. We'd barely spoken to one another in the last three years. Now here we were, alone together. I had never been alone with her before.

What should I say? Where to begin? The silence dragged on, became more and more uncomfortable the longer it lasted. And it wasn't just with Laura. I had trouble talking with girls in general. I had always been a pretty quiet kid in school. I could easily talk with my friends, Slow and Chimes and Pooch and the rest of the guys I'd known for years, but I never learned how to strike up a conversation with strangers or people I didn't know very well. I was impressed with others who could do that. At home I jabbered and joked constantly. My parents could never understand when my teachers described me as shy and quiet in class.

I needed to say something, anything, even if it was stupid. I asked Laura what classes she was taking at Minnisapa State. She responded enthusiastically; probably just glad we weren't sitting there in silence anymore. She told me in detail about each class, what they had done for the past two weeks, what her impressions of her professors were so far, and what she thought of the other students in her classes. I tried to concentrate on what she said but was distracted whenever I looked over at her. I figured I wouldn't remember any details of the things she said by tomorrow.

How could I tell her how I felt, how I had always felt, about her? It was hopeless. At the beginning of our junior year, she started dating a senior named Rick Nelson. Pooch and Slow had a field day making fun of his name, always behind his back, of course. Pooch would start singing *Garden Party* under his breath whenever Nelson appeared, and the rest of us would break up laughing. Nelson never had a clue. He was a typical jock, running back on the football team and starting forward in basketball. Tall, popular, a real jerk. Slow Slocum referred to him as a "Dube." It was amazing how much I hated him by the end of that year. I had heard he'd gone to college somewhere in Iowa. It didn't matter how far away he was; Laura was committed.

I was desperate. Things had never seemed this bad to me before. Why was I feeling so anxious? Maybe Laura was right. Maybe I was scared about leaving home.

Laura finished her spiel about her biology class. It included some funny story about her professor, but I don't remember it. Like I said, my concentration was shot. Then she asked if I knew what classes I'd be taking at the U. Once again, thankful to her for breaking the silence and asking me something I could talk about without thinking too hard. Comp, calculus, an intro literature class, I told her.

"Do you like English?" she asked.

"Yeah, I'll probably either major in that or math."

"You want to be a teacher, right?"

"Yeah." My dream was to become a writer someday, but teaching was my fallback plan. I wondered how she knew that. I'd certainly never talked to her about it.

"I was never very good in English," she said.

"Sure you were," I joked. "What about that speech you gave with the swords?" I enunciated the "w."

"You dork." She reached over and pushed my shoulder playfully. I couldn't remember a time that she'd ever touched me before.

Another few moments passed in silence. The ducks I had watched before had slowly made their way back to our side of the lake. Now the flock once again lifted from the water and flew off south. To the west I could see cars, tiny from this distance, driving on Marcotte Street where it crossed Lake Minnisapa. The sun almost touched the bluffs in the west. Not much daylight was left. It would be dusk soon.

Without preamble, Laura stood up and snapped her gum. "I suppose I should be going home, anyway."

She waited while I stood up. I walked her over to her bike where it stood next to the path. I wanted to take her arm while we walked or put my hand on the small of her back or around her shoulder, anything to make it feel like we were together. Instead, I stuck both my hands in the pockets of my jacket.

"Maybe I'll see you before you leave?" she said, making it a question. She swung her right leg over her bike.

"Yeah. Maybe I'll stop by Bridgeman's some night."

"Well, I don't waitress as often as I did this summer, because of school, you know, but I'll be there." She looked into my eyes. Her lips parted slightly. She was about to say something more, but she didn't. I don't know what she might have said then or what changed her mind. Lifting one of her pedals to the top of its circle with her foot, she pushed down. "Bye, Killer."

"See ya," I said. I watched her ride off. I was stunned. She had never called me that before. I didn't know she even knew about it. Not many people did. Slow and Pooch and that whole gang had decided sometime senior year that I needed a nickname, like most of them had. Chimes suggested a couple—Gramps, Pops, Carrot-Top—despite my hair being black, not red; I guess that was irony—but none of them caught on, thankfully. About two months before we graduated, Pooch came up with Killer. Since my last name was Gilmore, and Gary Gilmore's execution for murdering two people was all over the news, it struck him as funny somehow. When Pooch suggested it, Quint King happened to be sitting with us. I didn't really know Quint very well, he always seemed like trouble to me, and he looked like he was in some kind of drug induced haze at the moment, but he leaned over to Pooch and said, "Perfect." That was all it took. By graduation, I was Killer to all those guys. How Laura even knew about it, I had no clue. I know she didn't hang out with them, but her calling me that made me smile.

I stood on the path watching her ride away. She rounded a couple of curves where the path wound past the hospital. She looked back toward me. Her right hand lifted off the handlebars and I thought she was going to wave, but she quickly put it back. I supposed it was difficult to maintain control of her bike with only one hand, what with the mittens and all.

I walked back and retrieved my own bike. Right foot on the pedal, I swung my left leg over the bike, and headed off down the path, the opposite direction from the way Laura had taken. On the way home, my hands turned red from the cold.

4. A Life in Review

I n a sudden moment of clarity, I realized that I was completely upside down. I could feel the pressure of the restraining belt across my chest and left shoulder, tight even through my winter jacket. NRBQ's "Wild Weekend" blared loudly from the stereo speakers. Through the windshield all I could see was white, snow sprayed up from the car's tires into the air. Inside the car change flew up—or rather down—from the recessed holding area between the seats.

I had been driving on the Interstate, climbing a long, sloping hill. I came up quickly on a semi-trailer, moving very slowly in the right-hand lane. I shifted into the left lane and accelerated. I was anxious to get home, still an hour away. When I pulled even with the truck's cab, I hit a patch of ice, invisible on the highway's dark surface. My car started to slide. I knew I'd lost control. Undirected, it—I—slid left off the highway and into the wide median ditch between east and west bound traffic. (In that, at least, I was lucky. If the car had gone right instead of left, I would have been crushed beneath the truck's wheels.)

My headlights illuminated a landscape of unbroken white. This part of the state had received twelve inches of fresh snow in the past 24 hours on top of a foot or two that already covered the ground. The car plowed into the deep powder, quickly decelerating from the 50 or 60 mph I had been going on the highway. I clenched the steering wheel, though the car moved of its own accord. I skidded toward the middle of the ditch, waves of snow rising up over the right side of the car and covering the windshield. The car tipped on its right side, then flipped over, the roof contacting the snow-packed ground. Only a couple of seconds had passed since the car left the road, but time had slowed down for me.

The car continued to roll over, first my side, then the wheels, back on the snow. A bright flash of light through the windshield caused me to flinch, my eyes closed involuntarily, only momentarily, but when I opened them, I … I was still in the car, though back on the highway. No, I realized, this wasn't the Interstate, this was the county truck road that connected to the Interstate. I slowed down and stopped in the left turn lane. I waited for an approaching vehicle to move past before I could complete my turn. That turn would put me on the Interstate just a few hundred yards before the hill where I'd tried to pass the semi. I'd made this turn five minutes ago. The approaching car's lights were on the high beam setting, the light refracting on my windows. Was that the flash of light I'd seen through the windshield?

The car—actually a minivan—swished by, leaving a trail of swirling snow in its wake. I made the left turn onto the Interstate's onramp. Were the last five minutes a dream, a hallucination? How was I repeating what had just happened? Was this some strange déjà vu? As I merged from the onramp onto the Interstate, I breathed a sigh of relief. Whatever was going on, I was still safe in my car, with the wheels on the road, on my way home. I drove up the hill just as I had done—or imagined I'd done—five minutes earlier. Up ahead, a string of soft, red lights came into view. It was the semi. I gained on it as it crept slowly up the hill. No problem, I thought. I'd just slow down, follow the semi until it crested the hill. It wouldn't add more than a minute or two to my commute home. I smiled. Problem solved.

I was gaining on the semi quickly. I didn't—couldn't?—ease my foot off the accelerator. My left hand slid down the steering wheel and pushed down on the signal indicator. The turn signal started flashing. I gripped the wheel tighter. I couldn't stop what was coming. The car was moving past the semi, the patch of ice just ahead. I glanced down at the dashboard. The speedometer's red needle climbed higher. The glow of the dashboard's lights got brighter, filling my field of vision.

And I found myself staring at a glowing computer screen. What was this? I raised my head and looked around. My co-workers sat each in their own little cubicle, each wearing a headset, each staring at their computer monitor. I heard a steady tik tak of fingers flying across keyboards, and, just barely audible, the muted sound of Muzak playing an old Billy Joel song. I was back in the call center where I worked. I looked at the lower right corner of my computer screen. 7:10 p.m. Almost two hours until my shift ended, until I would get on the road and head home. Or the ditch, or wherever I might end up.

I started to shiver, and my shoulders shook. What was happening to me? I pushed my chair back and stood up. The words and numbers filling my computer screen didn't matter anymore. Two hours from now I was going to slide off the road at 50 mph into a snow-filled ditch and roll over. Could I change that, knowing what was coming? My recent experience—heading up the hill and overtaking the semi a second time—suggested I couldn't. Did I—or would I—die in that crash? The amount of fresh snow in the ditch might be enough to cushion the rollover. Maybe I'd walk away without a scratch. That sort of thing happened often enough, didn't it?

But why was I back in the call center? And how could I "remember" something that hadn't yet happened? I felt dizzy. My head swam.

A number of my co-workers were looking up at me. How long had I been standing? It couldn't have been more than a couple of seconds. I smiled weakly and nodded at my closest co-worker, Lynn. (Lynn, with her shoulder length black hair and deep, dark eyes, and infectious smile. She'd flashed me that great smile a lot lately, and I hadn't noticed her doing it to any of the others. And I had been paying attention. I thought about asking her out, but I hadn't yet. Yet. Was it too late now?) I patted my stomach and muttered, "Something I ate, I think."

I slipped past Lynn and made my way down the short hallway to the men's room. I turned the water on in the sink. I grabbed the sides of the basin and leaned forward. For a few moments, I just watched the water swirl down the drain. I wondered if I could change the future, knowing what was going to happen. I didn't remember making this trip to the bathroom before. Things could change then, I thought. But when I'd come up on the semi the second time, I hadn't intended to pass it, but I changed lanes anyway. Maybe I could take a different route home, avoid the Interstate altogether. That should work. And when I went back to my desk, I'd ask Lynn if she wanted to go out this weekend. That would certainly be a change in my future. Or my past, or whatever this was.

I looked up at my reflection in the mirror. I looked terrible, dark circles below bloodshot eyes. I'd soldier through the rest of my shift, then see if I could control which direction my car headed when I left. If I told Lynn, or anyone else, what was happening to me, they'd probably think I was crazy. Better to keep it to myself. I splashed cold water on my face and reached for the paper towels. The door behind me opened, and bright light from the hallway reflected off the mirror. Instinctively, I shut my eyes.

When I opened them a second later, I couldn't see anything. I sat up suddenly, only then realizing that I'd been lying down. I was on a couch, covered with a light blanket, wearing only a t-shirt and boxer shorts. My eyes slowly adjusted to the darkness, and I began to make out my surroundings. It was my brother Randolph's apartment. I'd visited Randolph earlier in the week—three days ago, I calculated—and stayed overnight. Now I was back there, more than two hundred miles from the call center, sleeping on his living room sofa, in the middle of the night.

"Oh, God," I whispered. I collapsed back onto the couch, throwing an arm over my face, covering my eyes. I felt a shift in temperature; the air was heavy with humidity and heat.

When I moved my arm, I was staring up at a star-filled night sky. I was far away from city lights and the Milky Way arced across my field of vision. A nearly full moon shone down on us. Us—I realized someone was lying next to me.

A light breeze picked up and the leaves in the trees above us swayed. The warm night told me it was summer. I could hear water lapping nearby. I was lying on a blanket, but I could feel the sand beneath it. The person lying next to me was more than just a vague presence that I sensed. An arm lay across my waist, a head rested on my chest. I looked down. The moonlight illuminated the long blond hair of the woman whose head lay gently on my chest.

Clare. This was Clare. If I was moving backward through time in my life, I'd made a big jump this time. Not only was it no longer winter, but it had been several years since I'd been with Clare. She stirred and lifted her head. She leaned over and kissed me gently, and then with more force, she thrust her tongue into my mouth. I returned her kiss, and my arms encircled her shoulders, my hands running over her bare back.

She was naked and so was I. My hands slid down to her hips and below. I lay on my back, and I could feel a stirring in my loins, so to speak. I realized where—and when—I was. Once on a summer night, Clare and I had crossed the bridge from our hometown to this small island in the middle of the river. We hiked to the far south end, hundreds of yards from where we'd left the car and farther than that from any other people. We made love on the beach underneath the moon and stars. It had been a magical night; a night I'd never forget. And I was there—here—again.

Clare pushed herself up on her elbows, ending our kiss. Her face only inches away from mine, she stared into my eyes. Hers were a light blue. "I love you," she said.

"I love you, too," I told her. And I did. I'd loved her when we were together, and all those feelings came rushing back into me now.

She kissed me again briefly. "I'm gonna go in the water," she said. That was Clare. Spontaneous. Carefree.

She stood, padded across the few feet of sand, and then she was in the river, the murky water swirling about her legs. I sat up and watched her. She waded out until the water was waist deep, then she dipped under the surface. She came up and ran her hands over her face and smoothed her wet hair back. The moonlight reflected off her pale skin. I stared at her breasts.

I loved her and I loved my life at that moment. I remembered everything about that night; I knew what was going to happen. In a moment, she'd come out of the water. We'd get dressed—our clothes lay in a scattered pile next to the blanket—and we'd go back to town, to her house, where I'd spend the night as I often did. I remembered how happy I'd been with her, and I wanted this moment to last. I wanted to stay where I now found myself.

She splashed water on her chest and stomach and rubbed her arms. I smiled, watching her. I glanced upward at the full moon. I couldn't believe how brightly it illuminated the river and the island. The moon seemed to grow in brightness and size, and I had to look away. I put a hand over my eyes.

When I pulled my hand away, it was dark. I was lying down still, but now I lay in a bed. My eyes adjusted once again to the darkness and I noticed a faint wavering light nearby. A window, heavily curtained. I sat up and pushed aside the fabric. The light came from a streetlamp on the corner and the flickering was caused by the branches of a tree that stood between it and the house. The branches were mostly bare, and the ground was littered with a collection of multi-colored leaves. Autumn now.

A quiet sigh and slight movement next to me drew my attention away from the window. I guess I'd known that I wasn't alone in the bed. A young woman—barely more than a girl—lay next to me, asleep but twitching while dreaming. She had short, light brown hair and wore a white T-shirt.

The blankets were up nearly to her shoulders. One arm flopped over to where I'd lain before sitting up.

Her name was Jasmine and we'd dated briefly when we were in college. I was a senior that year while Jasmine was only a freshman. This was her apartment which she shared with several other girls. I'd only spent a couple of nights here—she'd spent a few more at my place—but somehow, I was back in one of them. I'd been infatuated with her from the time we first met, but we didn't stay together very long. She transferred to another school after the first semester that year. We vowed to keep in touch, but we each sent only a couple of letters before we let it go. I'd never seen her again, and I met Clare the following spring just before graduating. My memories of Jasmine had almost completely faded away, but I still recalled her smile and the way she looked at me.

I gently moved her arm aside so I could lie back down. I watched her as well as I could in the darkness and listened to her breathing. I closed my eyes, wondering if I could fall asleep. I didn't want to wake Jasmine, and I didn't feel that I could get up from the bed or leave this room.

I didn't sleep, but lay awake a long time, listening to Jasmine breathe. When I closed my eyes, all I could sense was her lying next to me. The love we'd shared, however briefly, didn't come flooding back to me, the way mine and Clare's had earlier. I knew I'd loved Jasmine at the time, but maybe that love wasn't deep enough or hadn't lasted long enough for it to return. I'm not sure how much time passed while I lay there, but this was the longest I'd spent in one of my life's memories or regressions or whatever these were. And nothing was happening. Maybe that's why I stayed there; I had no idea how this worked. Maybe I was stuck here this time. Would I still be here in the morning when she woke up? I'd often wondered what might have happened to us if Jasmine hadn't moved away so soon after we met. I didn't try to talk her out of it. If I did, could I convince her to stay this time?

After some time, I started feeling dizzy. A dull ache and a throbbing began in my head. I started feeling nauseous as well. This all happened quickly, and I sat up in bed, feeling immediately like I might tumble out of it. Though my eyes were closed, I could tell it had become light beyond my eyelids. The soft comfort of the mattress had been replaced by something hard pressed against my buttocks. Something heavy and cool rested in my hands.

I opened my eyes. I sat on a wooden chair, holding a pitcher of water. The floor was tiled, and a series of mirrors and sinks stretched out before me. I heard voices talking and shouting somewhere nearby. Oh, my God, I knew what this was. Freshman year of college, I'd lived in a dormitory. The floor where I lived was exclusively male, and at the junction of two hallways was a large, communal bathroom with sinks, toilet stalls, urinals, and a shower area with a dozen or so shower heads. I was sitting on a desk chair in the middle of it.

One night that spring, I had gone out drinking with a bunch of the guys on my floor. I'd recently been rejected by yet another girl I'd met at school—my luck in that area had all been bad up to this point—and I'd gotten good and drunk for the first time in my life. When we returned to the dorm, my more experienced drinking companions told me that the only way to avoid a hangover the next day was to drink a pitcher of water before going to bed. They pulled a desk chair from my room into the bathroom, filled the pitcher I now held in my hands, told me to drink, and left me there alone.

Now the bathroom door swung open, and two of my night's drinking buddies burst in, laughing and yelling. "C'mon, man," shouted one of them who we called Eggman, a variation on his last name, "you need to drink that whole pitcher."

The other one—a short, mustachioed guy who I could only remember as Tim, who we then suspected, and later confirmed, to be gay—yelled "Bottoms up!" They were both pretty lit themselves and were much louder than they had any need to be. Plus, sounds echoed like crazy in this tiled bathroom. I winced. I've been drunk only a few times in my life, and this was the first time. I hadn't felt this way in a long time. I lifted the pitcher to my lips and took a long drink, while Eggman and Tim laughed.

I swallowed as much water as I could, then set the pitcher back in my lap. As memory served, I would drink this entire pitcher of water in the next few minutes. I don't know if that had anything to do with it or not, but I remember feeling just fine the next day, no residual effects from my night out. Right now, all I knew was that the lights in this room were much too bright, so I shut my eyes. As soon as I did, the sounds around me faded away to be replaced by the sound of crickets chirping on a summer's night. I could feel a pleasant breeze against my skin.

I tried lifting the pitcher of water again but realized that my hands were empty. My headache and nausea had disappeared along with the water pitcher. I leaned back. I felt comforted by the soft padding on the chair's seat and back. A warm breeze carried the scents of summer and the outdoors. Slowly I opened my eyes. The room was bathed in a soft, dim light that emanated from a small lamp. A bookshelf covered most of the opposite wall. It was filled with paperbacks and a few hardcover books. I recognized a lot of the titles, primarily old science fiction and fantasy books: Dune, The Lord of the Rings, Conan the Barbarian, Nine Princes in Amber, Asimov's Foundation series, several of John Norman's Gor books. The lower shelves held stacks of comic books. A narrow, single bed covered with a homemade quilt sat in the center of the room. A tall cabinet next to the bed held the lamp and a group of stereo components: a turntable, a receiver, a cassette tape deck. Next to the cabinet, an open window with white curtains that swayed in the soft breeze let in the sounds of the night: crickets, the cry of a nighthawk, cars in the distance. I sat in the corner next to the window, my feet propped up on the end of the bed. This was my room, my bedroom in my parents' house, the house where I'd grown up. This had been my room since the time I was five until I'd left for college.

I glanced out the window as I heard a car drive by. I watched the taillights as they disappeared past the house next door. The quiet sounds of a summer night returned. I ran a hand through my hair, which was full-bodied and long enough to brush my shoulders. I must have been about 16 or 17, during my high school years. This particular night didn't feel special in any way. I didn't remember it; I couldn't think of something that might have been about to happen. I wondered about that. Everything else—every time jump, every moment I'd experienced—had felt significant in one way or another. But I'd spent thousands of nights sitting in this room, just like this. If I strained, I could just barely hear the sound of the television from the downstairs living room. My dad was probably watching a movie or a baseball game. My mom might have been with him, sitting in her chair reading. I wondered if I could force myself, my younger self, to walk downstairs so I could see them again one more time. Given the time frame, they would have only been in their early fifties.

But I didn't get up. I didn't do anything. I just sat in the chair. What was the meaning of this? I know I'd suffered from depression as a teenager, though it wasn't discussed or even diagnosed back then. Everyone thought I was a happy kid, but I spent a lot of time in this room, lying on my bed reading comics or listening to albums, or exploring my new found sexuality. Is that what I was meant to get out of this— reminiscing about my adolescence? The thought that I was "meant" to get anything out of this experience sent my mind down a new corridor, or maybe down a black hole. Was there some intrinsic meaning behind what was happening to me? Was there an outside force controlling it? I'd been an atheist most of my adult life; was what was happening to me now beginning to change my mind?

Too many questions I didn't like and couldn't answer. I closed my eyes and put my hands over my face, fingers pressing tightly on my eyelids. I wanted to be out of here.

"Smile, honey," I heard my mother say. Had she come upstairs to my room without my hearing her?

I opened my eyes to find her standing in front of me. She looked young, not yet fifty, probably only in her early forties. She smiled. "Let's get a picture of you with your cake," she said. She lifted an old Polaroid instant camera to her face, looking at me through the viewfinder.

We were in the kitchen of our house, the same house where I'd just been sitting upstairs in my room. I was still sitting but now in one of the old wooden chairs that surrounded our kitchen table. I glanced down. I was holding a frosted cake on a plate on my lap. Tiny wax candles stood in a circle around its edges. A large number "8" was frosted in green in the center. Oh, my God, I realized where and when I was. This was my eighth birthday. I looked up at my mom. That ancient Polaroid camera she held was practically brand new.

"That's it," she said. "Now smile."

No, I wanted to scream at her but couldn't open my mouth. I just looked at the camera. She pressed the button, and the flash momentarily blinded me. I heard the whirr as the camera pushed the still developing picture out of the front slot. I knew the picture my mom had just taken; it had become a family legend: my eight-year-old self, holding my birthday cake, looking directly into the camera. But instead of looking happy, the boy in that picture looked very sad. My mom worried about that; she'd always tried to make our birthdays joyous and special occasions. Years later, my mom, my dad, my brother Randolph, everyone joked about that photo. My expression in that picture, the overwhelming sadness in my eyes, I looked trapped, lost. I was just a silly eight-year-old kid. But I always thought my eyes in that photo looked older, wiser, and infinitely sadder than any 8-year-old. It was creepy. And now I understood why.

My vision started coming back after the camera's flash, but the world looked brighter now. I felt as though I was moving. The world resolved into a green lawn and a couple of large shade trees. Beyond the trees, a couple of old cars cruised past on the street. I looked down and saw tiny hands holding the grips on the ends of a handlebar, a large wheel moving beneath it. Another glance revealed a pair of short legs furiously pumping up and down, moving pedals in a circle. Much of my life, I'd been a bicyclist, both for exercise and general transportation. But I didn't get my first bike until my tenth birthday. Besides, this was smaller, closer to the ground.

I rounded the corner of the house, and I knew where I was. My bedroom upstairs, with its sci-fi books and comics, had yet to be built (my parents had added the second floor to their house when I was five); the kitchen where I'd celebrated my eighth birthday was around the side of the house I'd just passed. I was outside, riding quickly around and around the house on my tricycle. I couldn't have been more than four years old, maybe only three. It was a simpler time, and playing outside alone, especially in one's own yard, was a common experience.

Around the next corner I cruised past the front door. It was summer. The sun beat down. I didn't care. I was riding my trike around and around the house. I was happy. My memories didn't reach this far back—my earliest childhood memories began around the age of five—but I recognized the house, the sidewalk, even my tricycle the way you remember something you've seen in pictures, even if the real-life memories are long gone. My adult mind in my child's body let go for a time, as I completed another lap around the house. This was fun. A sudden flash of memory came to me: telling my mom that I'd just ridden around the house one hundred times. I counted. Maybe I had and maybe I hadn't. Was this that day? I couldn't remember.

After another lap (I wasn't counting now), I began to wonder how long I'd stay in this moment, this memory, this time. My jumps didn't seem to follow any particular pattern. I'd been at the call center for maybe 10 minutes, Randolph's apartment for less than one. My time on the beach with Clare flew by, but it might have been as long as or even longer than I'd spent in bed next to Jasmine. The fact that I could remember those women—those experiences—while I rode my tricycle around my parents' house as a four-year-old struck me as absurd. I wanted to laugh, but my four-year-old self didn't.

A cloud moved in front of the sun and the day grew noticeably dimmer. I looked toward the street that went past the house. A semi-trailer rumbled by; this was before the city had built a cut-off that re-routed traffic away from this residential district. The sight of the semi reminded me of trying to pass one on the freeway and sliding off the road into the snow-filled ditch, the moment that started all this. I stopped riding as I watched the semi travel into the distance while another one approached from that direction. The day grew darker. I looked up into the sky, but the sun was completely obscured by clouds now. Still, it shouldn't have been this dark. The light faded until I couldn't see as far as the street anymore.

I tried to stand but couldn't feel the tricycle underneath me. I couldn't feel the ground. I was ... floating, maybe? The air around me felt warm. Then it didn't feel like air anymore, more like liquid. Was I floating in water ... or underwater? I couldn't see anything. I couldn't even tell if my eyes were open or closed. But it felt peaceful. I was content, more so than I'd been in a long, long time. Years, maybe decades. I felt like I could sleep. I felt like I could sleep for a long time. Was this the end of my journey? Or a beginning?

5. Siren

I *stand on the bank of the frozen river. In front of me stretches an unbroken white plain of freshly fallen snow over a thin layer of ice. The center of the mile wide river is open water, belying the sub-zero air temperature. A half mile to my left, down river, concrete pillars rise from the water and ice, holding the interstate bridge deck dozens of feet above. Cars rumble across the deck's grid, taillights receding into the west. Somewhere behind me, I hear a faint shout, from blocks away. Undoubtedly, the sound comes from a drunken college student, departing a local bar at closing time, not quite inebriated enough to hear the siren call from the river that I do. A car drives by on the street closest to me, its driver either ignoring or not noticing me. I stare out over the river.*

Liz first told me about the serial killer theory the night we met. About a dozen of us were crammed into my friend Matt's small one-bedroom apartment for an after-bars party. It was mid-March, about halfway through spring semester. The week before, a drowning death had shocked both campus and community. The local news media reported that a freshman student had wandered away from his friends after a night of heavy drinking, had wandered down to the river's edge, stumbled or fallen, and had been unable to save himself. His body was recovered two days later, bloated with river water. The official cause of death was listed as drowning. Blood alcohol levels were indeterminate after the body had been two days in the water.

I didn't think much more about the drowning, the death, before the night of the party, the night I met Liz. I was in my first year of grad school and was feeling overwhelmed between my own studies and teaching freshman comp. I was intimately familiar with the foolish, occasionally life-threatening, behavior of those younger than I. It hadn't been that long ago that I'd participated in some of those behaviors myself. We lived in the small Midwestern college town of

Bishop's Prairie; binge drinking was prevalent. Spring had come and the river was nearing flood stage. It could be a dangerous mix. These were facts. What I didn't know yet was that there was a pattern.

"Just think about," Liz was saying. I noticed her from across the room. She was an extremely animated, very attractive blonde girl. Sitting on the low chair in Matt's apartment, she looked small. Once I got to know her, I found out she was only 4'11". People thought of her as cute; I couldn't resist hugging her every time I saw her. She was a bundle of energy that could light up a room and capture everyone's attention. That was obvious to me from the moment I first saw her that night.

The other thing I noticed immediately was the silver crucifix necklace she wore. It was a gift from her late father; she wore it without irony, although she wasn't religious in any traditional sense, and never took it off, even when we made love. When she would brazenly—or so I thought of it—walk naked around the apartment we later shared, the crucifix would hang low between her ample breasts, reflecting whatever light the room provided.

"No, really think about it," Liz repeated. I made my way across the room, and joined the small circle of men and women over whom she held sway. She looked up at me as I approached, and I inclined my head, waiting for her to go on. "He wasn't the first victim," she said.

"Victim?" a skeptical young man with curly black hair and a full beard asked her.

"I've done the research," she continued. "Over the last several years, there have been four—now five—drowning victims in the river. All young men, all but one of them college students here in Bishop's Prairie."

"And all of them had been partying," another listener put in. I couldn't tell if she was adding to Liz's account or disputing her conclusion. As the volume of her voice rose on each syllable of the word "partying," shouts echoed through the room, and everyone other than me lifted their latest glass or bottle to their lips. I locked eyes with Liz and we shared a silent moment. I was desperate to hear her continue. I think I fell in love with her at that moment.

Here's what I learned from Liz then and afterwards: The first unexplained drowning occurred four years and eight months prior to that night. Nineteen-year-old Bobby Schlichter was celebrating the Fourth of July with his girlfriend Ellen and several mutual friends. After the fireworks display at the river's edge, a heated argument broke out between Bobby and Ellen. She felt—rightly so, it turned out—that Bobby had had too much to drink. Like most people who have had too much to drink, Bobby neither accepted the suggestion nor took too kindly to those who made it. He came close to taking a swing at her. Their other friends separated them and hustled her out of there, leaving Bobby alone. He remained behind on the riverbank while the rest of those who had attended the fireworks departed, making their way home. It was the last time anyone saw him alive. Twelve days later, his body was pulled from the river two miles downstream after being discovered by Eldon Schuh, who was out fishing in his boat.

Thirteen months later, another young man drowned in the river. And another, two months after that. The two deaths that year, coupled with Bobby Schlichter's the summer before, prompted a serious investigation. According to Liz, the FBI was even called in, although their investigators could find no connection between the three victims nor any evidence of foul play in any of the cases. All three men had been drinking heavily on the nights of their disappearances. The second fatality, like Bobby Schlichter, had been a college student and was seen in the vicinity of the river the night he disappeared. The third was the assistant manager of a local record store. He had closed the store on a Saturday night, then failed to report for work on Monday afternoon. A search and investigation followed. Several downtown bartenders, when shown his picture, remembered seeing him that Saturday night. Each said that he had drunk alone and left alone. No one was quite sure of the time. His body was found in the river later in the week.

"But we're not the only college town along this river," Liz was saying. She was right. The town of Kyona, thirty miles to the north on the opposite bank of the river, was nearly identical to our own. "They haven't had any mysterious drownings," she said.

"Wait a minute," a woman interrupted. She was an art major named Chelsea, a former girlfriend of my friend Matt. "Didn't a jeep go through the ice up there last winter?"

"It was two years ago," another listener, a redhead named Amy, put in. "Just after New Year's. All four people in the car died. My cousin knew one of the passengers."

"What about that?"

"Right," Liz responded. "Nothing mysterious there. The driver was drunk, missed a turn going too fast, and the car went through the ice. Complete explanation."

"But—?" Chelsea tried to begin.

"What happens here in Bishop's Prairie," Liz continued, cutting off any opposition, "is that a single person, always a young man, drowns in the river. It's usually someone who is drunk. Officially, they wander down to the river, usually by mistake, and fall in and drown, like they don't know where they are. Not a very convincing story."

"Have you been down to the river?" someone else asked. "No one swims in it. There's no beach."

"It would be pretty hard to just fall in by mistake," I added, wanting to be part of the conversation.

Liz looked into my eyes. A faint smile played around her lips. "Exactly," she said. "I can buy it happening—barely—once."

"Wasn't there a drowning down there last year about this time?"

Liz's eyes never left mine. "Yes," she said. "Number four. Last week's was number five."

Two and a half years had passed between the summer/fall of the double drowning and victim number four. Aaron Watts had been drinking at a local sorority party a week before spring break. He was hoping to get lucky that night. He didn't. Someone volunteered to drive him and a few other revelers home. When questioned independently, all three of the other people in the car at the time confirmed the location where Aaron Watts had been dropped off: near downtown, six blocks from the river. He told the driver that his apartment was nearby, though in truth he lived more than a mile and a half away. His body was recovered four days later.

Last week's freshman drowning made victim number five.

"Someone is killing these people," Liz said.

The snow crunches beneath my boots. The sound echoes over the river in the near silence. All the sounds of the city at my back have faded away. I don't hear cars. I don't hear voices. I don't hear dogs barking. I don't hear the hum of factories. Most everyone has gone home to sleep. My breath fogs in the sub-zero night air. In the cold and the silence, I can hear more clearly the call beckoning to me. I look across the river. The hills are dark. The lights and shadows of the bridge dance across the frozen waterscape. I step forward onto the ice.

It was five years ago when I first met Liz and first heard the serial killer theory. It was five years ago when I found out that that spring's drowning victim had not been the first unexplained death in the river. Five years ago, the river had claimed victim number five. If there had been other deaths earlier, others before Bobby Schlichter, we didn't know about them. No records existed of other mysterious drownings or unexplained deaths.

Four years ago, Liz and I shared an apartment that occupied one half of the second story of an old Victorian mansion about a mile from downtown and two miles from the riverfront. We became fast friends with the young married couple—Dave and Diane—who lived across the hall. We played cards or Monopoly or Scrabble on cold winter nights. We played disc golf on warm summer days. My grad school classes came and went in a blur of novels and literary theory. Liz was finishing her undergraduate degree in sociology. She debated between going into social work or going to law school. I counseled the latter; she had a keen, analytical mind and loved to do research. She loved cooking and experimented with new recipes. I rode my bike to school year-round and lost twenty pounds. Liz wormed her way past my defenses and brought me out of my carefully constructed shell. We made love in every room in the apartment. It was the happiest time of my life.

One Saturday afternoon while playing Frisbee golf at Regents Park, Dave said, "Did you hear about the kid who drowned in the river?" I don't know what made him think of it just then.

I froze on my backswing. Out of the corner of my eye, I saw Liz turn slowly and stare at Dave.

"Why do you have to bring something like that up?" Diane asked. "We're having a nice, fun day. You're impossible sometimes." The rest of us ignored her.

"When was that?" Liz asked.

Dave looked to Diane. "When was that, honey?"

She remained silent, staring out over the trimmed grass of the park.

"I guess a couple of months ago," Dave suggested.

Liz and I looked at each other. Neither of us moved. I breathed deeply. Birds flew from tree to tree. In the quiet, we heard a whoop from the sand volleyball players across the park. Liz and I'd been too wrapped up in our lives, too wrapped up in each other, to notice what was happening in the world outside.

"Are you going to throw or what?" Dave asked.

I looked down the course at the chain link basket hanging from a concrete pole that was the target for this "hole." I sighted along the line, drew my arm back then forward, snapping my wrist, and let fly the lime green disc I'd been using that summer.

"What happened?" Liz asked Dave. Her face looked drained of color; her gaze studious. I recognized that look. I'd seen her sit up all night, staring at her computer screen, or thumbing through the stack of books she kept by her side of the bed, searching for an answer to whatever question had possessed her.

"No one's really sure," Dave said. "This college kid—I remember now it was the week before their finals, last May, I suppose. Anyway, this kid disappeared one night, and they found him in the river the next day."

Dave managed an auto parts store in town. He didn't have much regard for the local college kids, other than as potential customers. He liked Liz and me, but that was about it. Diane tossed her bright blue Frisbee. This "hole" was a par three and Diane's disc landed just a couple of feet short of the basket that was our goal. She was the best player in our group and the most competitive. Dave and I enjoyed the game, but neither of us really cared who won. Liz just liked being outdoors. The four of us started walking to retrieve our discs for the second throw.

"Had he been drinking?" Liz asked.

Dave's laughter was deep and rich and long. "I did say he was a college kid, didn't I?"

Diane stopped, turned and looked at him harshly. "Can we drop this subject, please? I just want to have a nice Saturday afternoon, not talk about some poor, unfortunate kid who . . . died."

"Of course, honey. Sorry."

I looked over at Liz where she stood after picking up her red disc from the grass. The set of her shoulders told me that when we got home that night, she would devote herself to researching everything she could find about the drowning.

Victim number six.

The ice cracks beneath my heel. I pause. I hear something calling to me. It's not a voice, not exactly. I need to keep moving. The ice gets thinner closer to the center of the river. The water current is slow but steady. I look behind me. I see a single set of tracks—footprints—in the newly fallen snow: Mine. The lights of the city have faded in the cold night air. I turn and look toward the center of the river. I step forward.

Three years ago, Liz and I were fighting a lot. It started that spring and intensified over the summer. She would go days speaking to me in only short, clipped sentences, if at all. Usually, I didn't even know what we were fighting about. Small things would set her off; often I didn't know what set her off. One night during an argument, she threw a ceramic plate down on the counter, shattering it. As she stormed out of the kitchen, she swept a glass off that same counter, sent it hurtling to break against the wall. In the heavy silence that followed, I cleaned up the bits of broken glass from the counter and floor. In the morning, she looked like she wanted to apologize, but couldn't bring herself to do it.

I had completed my graduate program in English and was working part-time in a local bookstore, deciding what to do next. Pursuing a PhD wasn't out of the question, but I wanted to take some time off first. My hours at the store were mostly evenings and weekends and the pay was low, but I was in my element, surrounded by words on paper. Liz had finished her sociology degree and was looking into law schools. She failed the LSAT, the law school admission test, but didn't tell me about it until I saw the results sitting on her desk one morning. She yelled at me for going through her stuff and stormed out of the apartment. She was still gone when I left for work at 5:00 p.m. I started to realize that something more than me was making her angry, though I still didn't know what that was.

Silas Johnson grew up in a very poor neighborhood on the south side of Chicago. Standing 6'4", his height and athletic ability helped him to escape on a basketball scholarship. He was a starter by the end of his freshman season and garnered national attention as a sophomore. When the leaves turned color and autumn brought cool winds, Silas eagerly anticipated the start of another season. One weekend in late October, he and several of his teammates celebrated Silas's twenty-first birthday by wandering downtown from bar to bar. By Monday morning, rescue crews were dragging the river. Monday evening, Silas's body was pulled up.

All of this was reported in the media accounts that week. I showed the first article that appeared to Liz. We spent the rest of the week scouring the paper together and watching the evening newscasts on nights I wasn't working. Though more morbid than pleasant, it was the first time in months that Liz and I had done something together that didn't involve an argument. By the next week, the story had run its course, and the news crews had moved on to something else. Liz filed everything away into that secret, obsessive compartment in her mind.

One night a couple of weeks later, I tried to bring it up to Liz. "He fits the profile," I said. Liz sat in a stuffed armchair that Dave and Diane had given us when they moved out that summer, reading a hardcover novel I'd brought home from the store. She didn't respond.

"Young, male. He'd been drinking," I added.

She flipped a page in her book without looking up.

"He was the first black man," I said. "The first African American victim. Do you think that's significant?"

Then she looked up at me with a withering glance. She frowned, shook her head almost imperceptibly, and returned to her book.

The week before Thanksgiving, Liz left me.

The ice is thinner near the center of the river. It cracks loudly underfoot. The echoes bounce off the hills. I step forward gingerly. I don't look back anymore now. The city is behind me. That life is behind me. It's over. I can hear the current. I approach the center. I hear open water lapping at the edges of the ice. I can hear my name being called.

Two years ago, I was sitting in my usual booth at McGowan's Irish Pub when I heard my name called. I raised my head and saw a woman crossing the room toward me. She was of medium height, medium build, and had short, dark hair. She plopped herself down across from me.

"How are you?" she asked.

I recognized her. She had lived across the hall from me when Liz and I had shared an apartment. I hadn't seen her in more than a year.

"Diane," I mumbled.

She smiled. "Well, at least you remembered my name. Buy a girl a drink?" She flagged down a waitress and ordered a gin and tonic. The waitress asked if I wanted another beer. I nodded.

Diane reached across the table and took my hand. "How are you?" she repeated. Her eyes reflected neon bar signs and showed genuine concern.

"Drunk," I said, hoisting my beer.

She laughed a bit too loudly. The waitress brought our drinks.

"No, really," she said, "how have you been?"

"Drunk," I repeated, chuckling.

Diane didn't laugh that time, or even smile.

"I heard about Liz," she said. My smile faded, and I took a swallow from my new bottle. The beer was cold and bitter. "That sucks," she said. "You two always seemed so happy."

"We were," I said. She and Dave had moved before Liz and I started fighting.

"That sucks," she repeated. "What happened?"

I shrugged, drank.

"Doesn't matter," she said. "You don't want to talk about it. That's okay. What's new? Are you still working at the bookstore?"

"Yeah," I nodded. "Part time." I spent a lot of the rest of my time here at McGowan's. I didn't bother telling Diane that.

"I suppose you heard about Dave and me?"

I looked up at her, shook my head.

"We split up, too. We're separated."

"What happened?"

"Cheated on me," she said matter-of-factly. "Just once, I think, but that was enough. I wasn't going to stand for that."

It was my turn to say it: "That sucks."

"Tell me about it. So I come home one night—this was long after we moved out of the building where we lived across the hall from you and Liz, after we had our own house, you know—anyway, I come home and I find this, you know, a hair scrunchie thing, in the bathroom. Well, I knew it wasn't mine, so I asked him, whose is this? What's it doing in our house?"

"What'd he say?"

"Well, first he denies it. Swears up and down he doesn't know whose it is, where it came from, what it's doing in our bathroom. Finally, I get him to admit it. He breaks down, he's crying, you know? But, yeah, he had some girl over. In our own goddamn bed, can you believe it?"

"Man."

"Then he tries to defend himself, like he's not getting enough from me. Whatever. I gave him everything I could. I used to... Well, I won't stand to be disrespected like that."

"Yeah, no, you shouldn't."

"Well, I won't. Anyway, I'm in tears by this point. He tries to put his arms around me. I just told him to get out."

"Wow."

"Anyway, that was months ago. We separated. He moved out."

"Are you … getting … divorced?"

"Yeah, it's in the works."

Somehow, we ended up back at my apartment. Diane picked out a Bob Marley CD from my collection and we sat together on the couch.

"I know what I should tell you," she said suddenly, eagerly. "I remember how you and Liz were really interested in these stories. You probably heard about the guy who drowned in the river last month?"

I hadn't. The news took a bit of the buzz off.

"I knew him," she continued. "I started waitressing down at Tony's Pizzeria after Dave and I split. I needed to pay the rent, you know, and bills. Anyway, this guy—this kid—worked there on the weekends. He was a part-time cook. Ernie. Nice kid. I think he had kind of a crush on me, but he was only like eighteen, nineteen, you know? A college student. We had a good time. We flirted back and forth with each other a lot. But it didn't mean anything, you know. Just fun. Anyway, about a month ago, he disappears. Three, four days go by, nobody sees him or hears from him. One night I go into work and everyone's really down. Judy—the other waitress—is just sitting at a table, in tears. Tony tells me they found Ernie in the river. He'd drowned. Just like that other kid a couple of years ago."

"That other kid …?"

Diane hadn't been following things the way Liz had. The way I did after meeting Liz. I knew what Liz would say: victim number eight.

Diane had leaned against me while she told her story. Absently, I put an arm around her. She took my hand in hers. With my other hand, I stroked her arm up and down as she spoke. When she finished her story, she turned to look at me. Our faces were only inches apart. I bent forward. We kissed for a while. I fell asleep on the couch. When I woke up later, Diane had gone.

As I draw nearer the open water, the ice becomes thinner. Beneath my feet the cracks spread farther and more rapidly than before. My hair is stiff and brittle, frost-covered and frozen. My sinuses drain and freeze in the sub-zero air. A sharp intake of breath makes my teeth ache. My mind is clear and focused. I take another step forward and I hear a chunk of ice break free and fall into the freezing water. I stagger for a moment. It's hard to keep my balance. In the pure silence of the night, I hear the river calling to me. I hear my name spoken. My mind is clear and focused.

Just over a year ago was the last time I heard Liz's name. I was walking home from the bookstore on a late Saturday afternoon. Winter was late in coming that year, but autumn had nearly given up its grip. A chill wind blew steadily from the north that day. I spotted my old friend Matt rounding the corner ahead of me. I hadn't seen or spoken to him in months. He carried a manila folder under one arm with some papers sticking out. I suggested coffee and getting out of the wind. Matt opted for a beer at the nearest bar instead. I was drinking less than I had in the two years prior, but I hadn't given it up completely.

We talked over what we'd each experienced in the months since last we'd communicated. I didn't have much to say. Outside the bookstore, I read a lot. I'd taken up riding my bike again that summer. No, I wasn't dating anyone. Matt was working in a medical lab of some type at the hospital. I didn't quite understand his job, and he didn't quite explain it. I remembered that it was at his apartment that I first met Liz. I mentioned her and the party.

"Yeah, I kinda remember that," Matt said. "That was what, five years ago?" He placed his hand almost protectively on the folder of papers he'd set on the table.

"Four," I said. "Right after I came to B.P. My first year of grad school."

"And that was the first time you met her? Liz?"

I nodded.

"I didn't realize that," he said.

"You knew her before that, didn't you?"

"She and I had some class together. I don't even remember what it was. You guys were together a long time, weren't you?"

"Two-and-a-half years," I answered. I realized then that it had been over two years since we'd broken up, since Liz had left me. Almost as long as we'd been together. "I still miss her," I said.

"This is weird," I continued. "I just—I was thinking about this just last night for some reason. This is kind of weird." I stared past Matt into the dim recesses of the bar as I talked. "When we slept together—I mean, really slept—we used to lay back-to-back a lot. In the summertime, we didn't have air conditioning in our apartment, and it would get so hot, and her back would press up against mine, her butt would press up against mine. It would feel so hot and sweaty and uncomfortable. I hadn't really slept with anyone before that. It made me—I would get so annoyed. Now I think about that and miss it." I took a swallow of my beer, and looked back at Matt. "I don't know what made me think of that, but isn't it weird?"

He didn't say anything.

"Do you still see her?" I asked. "Liz?"

He took a drink before he answered. "Yeah. I see her around sometimes." He looked uncomfortable.

"Do you know what she's doing these days?"

"She works for the county. Social services."

I nodded. That would be Liz. Matt fidgeted. I decided to change the subject.

"What's with the papers?" I asked.

"Oh. Nothing. Just some stuff I picked up from the library," he said. "Research."

"Library research? Sounds important. Something for work?"

"No, it's ... nothing." He picked up the folder and waved it casually.

"Mind if I take a look?"

"It's just that my printer's not working at home, so..."

"So what is it? Something I shouldn't see?"

"No, no. Of course...here." He shrugged and pushed the folder across the table.

I flipped it open, started leafing through the pages. They consisted of newspaper stories, internet printouts, background information. There was even a copy of a police report. Jacob Holmes had drowned in the river two weeks before. I knew the story.

Jacob was only seventeen, still in high school. A bright kid, honors student. Involved in speech, theatre, debate. He ran cross-country. He played bass in a punk rock band. He'd gone to a party one night, drank heavily. *I'd never seen him drink before*, one of his friends had said. *He was totally wasted.* No one saw him leave the party.

I pushed the folder back across the table to Matt. "What's your interest in this kid?" I asked.

Matt shrugged. "Lots of people have drowned in the river," he said. "Over the years."

A prolonged silence followed.

"Liz—" I began.

"Listen—" Matt said at the same time.

We both stopped. I laughed humorlessly. Matt smiled uncomfortably.

"I got this stuff for Liz," he said. "She's really into it. You know that," he added, his voice quiet.

Though he was younger than the others, Jacob fit the profile. Victim number nine, Liz would say. She was still collecting stories about those who drowned in the river, still working on theories about their deaths. I shook my head . It was something we had shared, the only connection we still had.

"She thinks there's a serial killer," Matt said.

"I've heard the theory," I told him. "Don't you?"

He shrugged again. "I don't know. It's just strange is all."

I picked up my beer bottle. It was empty. Matt's was too. It was time to either order another round or to leave.

"Listen," Matt said. "I have to tell you something. Liz and I—we're together. We're seeing each other."

I nodded. Matt squirmed in his seat. "I thought you should know," he said.

I looked up at him. "Is she happy?" I asked.

"Yeah," he said. "I think she is."

Outside on the sidewalk, Matt said, "Listen, man, I'm sorry."

"It's okay," I said, cutting him off. I put a hand on his shoulder. "It was over a long time ago."

Matt nodded, turned, and walked up the block. I continued on my way alone, back home to my empty apartment.

I stand on the cusp of open water. The toes of my boots jut over the edge. The ice below my feet groans painfully. It cannot hold my weight much longer.

I hear the voice call to me, call my name. It wants me. The wind picks up, but I no longer feel it. I no longer feel the cold. It wants me. It loves me.

Come, *the voice says to me.* Jump.

My mind is clear and focused.

I know what Bobby Schlichter knew. What Silas Johnson knew. What Aaron Watts and Ernie and Jacob and all the others knew.

It wants me. It loves me. It will protect me.

Come.

I step forward and slip below. The water is cold.

The water is warm.

The water is cold.

6. The Amazing London Teleportation Device

"We should go to London," Melissa said.

We'd been watching TV in the upstairs room that served as our office during the day. In the evenings, after Melissa had finished her work for the day and I'd given up any pretense of trying to write, the office converted to our entertainment room. We'd sit with a large bowl of popcorn—organic, of course—and watch a movie or one of the few TV shows we shared an appreciation for. I drank Dr. Pepper or Orange Crush; Melissa usually opted for a glass of red wine.

We tried our best to ignore the commercial interruptions, but something about this particular one caught our attention. I grabbed a handful of popcorn; Melissa set down her wine glass. An upbeat instrumental tune—electric guitar, Fender Rhodes piano, swirling organ, and the slightest touch of saxophone—played over scenes of various places, both exotic and quotidian. The video showed a tropical beach at sunset, snow-capped mountains, a jeep climbing over sand dunes, endangered animals loping through the jungle, a couple snuggling one another during a gondola ride in Venice, fireworks over what might have been Tokyo, and finally, a red double decker bus cruising past an urban castle.

That was when Melissa said, "We should go to London."

"Hmm. Maybe someday."

That was eight years ago.

She turned and looked at me. "Sorry, honey. Sometimes I forget."

I smiled and kissed her. "I'm glad you can forget," I said.

Legal issues prevented me from leaving the country. I didn't like to talk about it.

"Besides," I said, "when's the last time you took a vacation from work? More than a day or two?"

"I know," she nodded. Melissa had taken a trip to New Zealand a few years ago, but that was before I'd met her. In the years we'd been together, she never took time off, except for a day here or there, maybe a long weekend. She was a workaholic. My viewpoint was different. If I managed four hours of writing in the morning, I considered it an extremely successful day.

"Still," she said, wistful.

Then our show came back on, and the subject was dropped, forgotten.

Eight years later, we were on a flight over the Atlantic, on our way to London. New York City was far behind us, as were my legal issues. Melissa relaxed, sipped wine, and enjoyed the view out the windows. I drank outrageously expensive beer and read an entire 562-page novel during the flight.

We landed at Heathrow Airport and took a taxi to the Strand Palace Hotel, "in the heart of London's West End." After checking in and a short nap, we went out for a light dinner. The next two days were devoted to sightseeing: Westminster Abbey, the Tower of London, the Globe Theatre. We rode the London Eye and visited Madame Tussauds. We took a double decker bus tour. It was all very lovely, fun, entertaining, and touristy, but in the end, it was all just a way of passing the time until our trip to Islington and our ultimate destination.

We took the London Underground—the tube—to Angel station, Islington, and walked a few blocks to the N1 Centre. Across the street from the massive shopping plaza rose a relatively new building, the Williams & Keye Department Store. W&K stood six stories tall, the first two devoted to retail sales. The third floor, I would find out later, mainly housed administrative offices, and four and five were used for storage. Below ground, a basement was used for more storage; and under that, a two-level sub-basement held the equipment needed to power and run W&K's single greatest attraction.

The Amazing Teleportation Device had been in operation for a little over six months. Scientists, engineers, and scholars all hailed it as one of humanity's greatest achievements, a machine that could transport physical objects—including human beings—from one location to another. Some journalists enthused about the potential benefits in energy and environmental savings. Others cautioned that possible military uses outweighed the advantages. From a purely theoretical standpoint, it definitely stood as one of the most amazing breakthroughs in human history. W&K saw it as the ultimate adventure park ride and an unparalleled profit engine.

Melissa and I had come to London specifically to experience the Amazing Teleportation Device. They'd designed the "ride" to transport people from W&K's main sales floor—where they had cleared out a large space in the center of the room for the unit—to the otherwise unused sixth floor of the building, where a receiving unit had been installed. The store was crowded when we arrived. Some people shopped for their everyday household items, while others flocked around the Device, whispering, pointing, and admiring. Still others looked at it with fear in their eyes. The area around the Device was roped off using one of those velvet-ropes-and-metal-stanchions things. It wouldn't have kept anyone out if they'd wanted to get closer to the machine, nor would the lackluster, minimum-wage security guards, who milled about looking bored. But no one pressed closer. Everyone was either impressed or frightened, or some combination thereof.

We stood in line and waited for our chance to experience something few human beings ever had. The line was surprisingly short considering the number of people in the store, but then again, this experience was far from cheap. W&K knew what they had and charged appropriately for it. Once again, as often in the past, I was grateful for Melissa's job and the income she pulled in. And more so for the fact that she was willing to share with me.

An announcement was made that those not participating—that was the word they used—in the Amazing Teleportation Device today would need to exit before they could begin. People started moving toward the exit, which for a moment caused it to become more crowded where we stood. I felt someone grab and squeeze my buttocks. I turned and looked around but couldn't tell who had done it. The crowd pressed toward the doors. I laughed and shook my head. Melissa looked at me questioningly. I told her what had happened, and she pressed her lips together. She didn't find it as humorous as I did.

Finally, after an interminably long time, the room was reduced to a few dozen people, those of us who had paid for the privilege of having our bodies teleported five stories upward. We slowly advanced forward past the velvet ropes and a smiling middle-aged man in an expensive suit calmly took each of our tickets and passed it through a computerized scanner. The tickets were printed on a special material with embossed lettering and a special ink that couldn't be duplicated, or so I'd been told. Early on some people attempted to pass through with forgeries, but nothing of the sort happened anymore. Our entire group eventually passed through security and assembled on a large platform surrounded by towering machinery with flashing lights. I wondered how much was necessary for the actual journey and how much was designed to look impressive for the consumer. Maybe I'm too cynical.

We were welcomed once again to the Amazing Teleportation Device and endured a thankfully short spiel about the wonders of W&K's marvelous invention. We were asked if we were ready to teleport and a cheer went up from the assembled crowd. It was a bit like being at a sporting event, or a fabulous new carnival ride, which I suppose is what it was.

"Now," the instructions continued, "if you're here with someone—and I'm pretty sure everyone is today—especially if it's someone special, you might want to hang on to one another as the machine takes you away. It's not necessary, but if you've never experienced teleportation before—if today is your first time with the Amazing Teleportation Device—it will make it a little easier on you."

I wondered if anyone in our group was not doing this for the first time. The faces I saw revealed mostly excitement, mixed with a bit of fear or at the very least trepidation. I didn't think anyone here was a return customer.

We were told, again, that it wasn't dangerous, and no one had ever been hurt by the experience, but that occasionally, rarely, someone felt a bit of nausea on arriving at the sixth-floor landing pad. That's what they called it, the "landing pad."

"All right, one last bit of advice, and this is an odd one. I want everyone to think about the color yellow; that's right, yellow; just concentrate on that color, keep it in your mind. We don't know why—this part's still a mystery to us—but thinking about yellow makes the transition smoother. Okay, everyone, think yellow and here we go!"

I was less intrigued with how the thought of yellow, or any color, for that matter, would make the transition easier than how someone had managed to figure that out in the first place. I began to say something to Melissa, but suddenly there were lights flashing all around us and a humming started. The chatter of voices around us rose as well. The humming sound faded away, or maybe just went subsonic. I could feel my eardrums pulsing and my clothes vibrated. It felt like being at a rock concert, standing in front of a wall of speakers, and feeling the bass notes ripple through my jeans. I had to admit I was even more excited than I'd thought I'd be.

I remembered then that I was supposed to think about yellow and so I did, filling my mind with an image of that color just stretching out before me to the horizon. I started to feel dizzy. I leaned to one side—I think I did, anyway. I couldn't see anything—my field of vision was a never-ending stretch of yellow. It seemed suddenly impossible to stand up anymore. I was unable to keep my balance; I began to fall over. Again, that's how I remember it. At the time, there was nothing in my sight but the color yellow. As I began to fall, I felt a strong pressure on my arm and my back, my shoulder and side as well. Someone was holding me upright. Melissa, I assumed. I felt safe, confident, secure in her hands. Maybe her arm was around my shoulder. I might have smiled then; who knows?

That was when I lost consciousness.

That wasn't supposed to happen.

I came to, my eyes fluttering open. There were people standing above me. I was prone, lying on a hard surface. Several people were looking my way, concern on their faces. I thought I recognized them from the group that had assembled on the teleportation platform. A young man cradled my head in his hands, rested on his lap. A young woman knelt above me. She held one of my hands in hers. Her other hand rested on my forehead, then stroked my cheek. She looked into my eyes. She looked worried.

"He's coming around," someone said, the young man who held my head.

"Are you all right?" the young woman asked, her face showing some relief now.

"I'm fine," I said, my voice a bit hoarse. "What happened?"

"You passed out," she said. Her smile was conciliatory. "It happens sometimes."

"Ah," I said. I glanced around as best I could. "Melissa?" I asked.

"Melissa?" the woman repeated.

"The woman he came in with," the young man answered her.

"Oh," she said. The look of worry was back on her face, amplified this time.

A bit later, I was seated in an office, holding a cup of tea. A blanket draped over my shoulders, though I didn't feel particularly cold. Several people stood nearby, dressed in suits and ties, looking nervous. Lawyers, I figured. Behind a rather imposing desk—I noted that it was devoid of any clutter: just a small, framed picture of two children and an ancient looking phone—sat a rather large man. Balding, with jowls that flopped over the collar of his starched shirt, he looked extremely uncomfortable. He looked at the others in the room—looked to them for advice, I thought. But to a person, they either looked away or down at their notes or phones. One coughed and fixed his gaze out the window. I could see buildings, London. I was where I was supposed to be. Melissa was not.

"So," the large man began, and cleared his throat. "There was a problem."

I set my cup of tea, half finished, on his desk in front of me. He scowled briefly, then realized he had bigger problems to deal with. "A problem?" I repeated.

He took a deep breath, resigned to start again. "My name is Mr. Keye," he said.

"Keye? Of Williams and Keye?"

"Yes, quite."

"You're the owner of the store?"

He puffed himself up. "President of the company, yes," he said.

"Then I would say you do have a problem, Mr. Keye." He scowled again and opened his mouth, but I continued before he could speak. "Where's Melissa?"

"Well, the good news is we know where she is."

"And the bad news?"

"Oh, not to worry, sir. She's quite all right."

"Just not here?"

He sighed. "The Teleportation Device—Malfunctioned."

"Malfunctioned?"

"I assure you nothing like this has ever happened before."

"Doesn't make me feel better. Where's Melissa?"

"Ah, well. Right. She arrived about 70 miles away."

"She was teleported 70 miles?"

"It's really quite astonishing. We had no idea the device could function at anything like that level. We're going to have to look at this in a whole new light."

"I'm sure you will. But ... Melissa? She's okay?"

"Oh, yes, no harm done. Apparently."

"Can I see her? Speak to her?"

He raised his hand. "Not to worry, sir. We can send you to go fetch your daughter momentarily."

"Really?" I said. I think I may have raised my voice then. I'm not sure. "Do I really look that much older to you?"

Keye stared at me. Obviously, this was not the reaction he was expecting.

I shook my head. "Melissa's not my daughter. She's my wife."

"Oh, I see. Quite right, sir. Sorry."

Actually, that wasn't quite the truth, either. Although Melissa and I had been living together for the better part of a decade now, we weren't married. A wedding had been planned years ago. A lot of tension had built up in the weeks leading to the planned wedding, particularly involving Melissa's two sons. One night we were having dinner with the two boys, who would have been 18 and I guess 21, at the time, adults, at least chronologically. The youngest, Joshua, became visibly upset, more so as dinner went on. I wasn't quite sure what was going on. He might have been worried about losing his mother to this new man in her life, whatever. His older brother, Owen, egged him on mercilessly, taunting him at every possible opportunity. From what I'd observed even at that early juncture, that seemed to be the regular dynamic between the two of them. The more I got to know them, the more my early observations proved right.

That night, as Joshua became more and more agitated, he grabbed a glass of beer from the table—it wasn't his, maybe Melissa's, more likely Owen's—and swung his arm back and forth. Beer spilled on the table, over Owen, onto the floor, everywhere. He slammed the glass on the table and jumped up. He came around the table, heading straight toward me. I admit to being worried for my safety at that moment. I hadn't spent much time with Joshua up til then—he lived with his dad when Melissa and I'd gotten together, but I knew he was unpredictable, quick-tempered, flying into a rage one moment but completely calm the next. And I knew he could be violent. I tensed up.

But he didn't touch me; he just yelled. "Don't you understand what matters to me?" That's the phrase I remember, that stuck in my mind. He repeated it several times before stalking off, leaving the dining room, leaving the house. Melissa helped Owen get cleaned up and together they cleared the table and wiped the floor. Neither of them talked about it; that was their way. I just sat there stunned. The incident led to a long estrangement between the two boys. I think a year passed before they spoke to each other again.

Meanwhile, wedding plans continued; it was to be a small ceremony in the backyard of the house with just a few friends. The night before, Melissa and I called it off. An old friend of Melissa's was visiting—she might have been a distant cousin; I was never entirely sure of the relationship—and she suggested to Melissa some changes, ways she thought the ceremony could be improved, made better. Melissa seemed enthused. Did I mind postponing the wedding, she asked me, just for a short while. No, of course I didn't, whatever she wanted. Things were delayed and delayed again. Obstacles came up. It never happened. Eventually, we just forgot about it.

Melissa and I had been together longer than most of the married couples we knew. And we were happier than most of them, as well. I didn't feel like telling any of this to Mr. Keye, however.

"It was my wife's idea to come to London, to experience your Teleportation Device in the first place."

"Yes, of course, sir. I find that it is often the wife who forces her husband to try the Device."

"Melissa didn't force me," I said. My anger was rising now.

"Sorry again, sir. A poor choice of words on my part."

"You know where she is?" I asked again.

"Yes, yes, of course we do. It's a quaint little village, very rural. Lots of—what do they have there?" he asked one of his associates.

"Chickens, mostly, sir," he responded.

"Ah, yes, right," Keye said. "Chickens. And from what I understand some very odd specimens, as well."

"Indeed, sir."

"Chickens?" I said. "That's … odd." Keye looked at me questioningly. "Melissa has chickens at home. She raises a few to sell eggs at the Farmers' Market."

"Really, sir? Indeed." Keye looked down, ran his hands along the top of his desk, lost in thought. "I wonder if that had anything to do with her getting lost, her ending up where she did. Interesting. Let's look into that."

One of his associates made a note.

I cleared my throat. "But you're bringing her back here? To London?"

"We could send someone to pick her up, of course, sir, and we'll do that. However, I think the best thing to do at this point is to send you to her, sir. I'm sure she has no idea what's happened, and seeing you arrive would be the best thing for her. And all around."

I nodded. "Okay."

"So, two options. We can send you there overland, but that's going to take some time. You need to get out of the city and then there's some rough terrain just before you get to the village."

"Option two?" I asked, thinking of a helicopter ride, which might turn out to be kind of relaxing at this point.

"We teleport you there."

"What?"

"The Teleportation Device."

"But I thought you said..."

He looked to one of his other associates, a middle-aged woman who stepped forward and spoke. "We think, sir, that we can send you through the Device again. I've spoken with the Controllers, those in the know and such, and they believe that knowing where she is and given your close, personal connection, they can send you directly to her."

"It's really the best way," Keye put in, excited. "We send you right to her. And everything's okay."

Everything's okay, I wondered. It sounded like he was trying to convince himself or his lawyers more than me. I'm sure potential lawsuits had been discussed. I didn't really care about that just then; I just wanted Melissa back. The plan was I would arrive, assure Melissa that everything was okay, and someone would show up by car later in the day to bring us back to London.

And so it was a short time later, I found myself standing once again on the platform of the Amazing Teleportation

Device. To say I was nervous would be the understatement of the century, no, of the millennium. The first time I'd been here, I'd passed out and lost my wife (okay, my partner, you know what I mean). And that was just moving five stories straight up. Now they intended to send me 70 miles away. But this was for Melissa.

"Are you ready?" they asked me.

"Yes. Yes, I think so. I just think about yellow …?"

"No, not this time. Think about your wife, sir."

"Of course."

"Concentrate on your feelings for her, your relationship. Think about what she looks like, her appearance. Just keep her foremost in your mind."

That wouldn't be hard to do. She'd already been there for years. I tried to control my fear and think about Melissa, concentrate on happier times.

The humming started, louder this time without the voices of other people around me. I closed my eyes but could still sense the flashing of lights. Had they ever done this with a single individual before? Or tried on purpose to send someone this many miles away? I should have asked more questions before I got on the platform.

I opened my eyes. Lights flashed, red, blue, amber. After a moment, the colors started to fade. Soon everything was white. Nothing existed around me but a vast whiteness in every direction. I looked around, up, down, side to side: nothing but white. I floated in a vast sea of nothingness.

Then, in an instant, I felt the pull of gravity, and I hit the earth with a shock. It knocked the wind out of me, but I wasn't hurt. I could feel dirt, grass underneath my head, my hands. A chicken, a normal-looking, yellow feathered chicken, pecked at the ground not three feet from me. I sat up. Clusters of people stood around, all looking at me. They were dressed simply, in a somewhat rustic fashion. No suits or ties, like the lawyers in Keye's office. Somebody might have murmured "Another one," but maybe that was just in my head. I heard a sharp intake of breath and across the field from where I sat, she stood. Melissa. She had one hand raised to her mouth, and her eyes went wide, fixed on me. She broke into a smile.

I did too.

7. Paper

Jacobus Quillen impressed me when he first appeared in my office. He was a small, slender man wearing an old-fashioned tweed jacket and cap. He carried a black leather satchel. He removed the cap when he entered my office. My assistant Amy introduced him as "Jacob Quillen" after announcing via intercom that I had an unscheduled visitor. I didn't have any pressing business that needed to be completed by the end of the day, and feeling rather bored, I'd asked her to show him in.

"Jacobus Quillen," he corrected her, while tucking his cap under the arm that held the satchel, and simultaneously extending his other hand to me.

I stood, reached across my desk to shake hands, and said, "Mr. Quillen. Please take a seat."

A large table and eight chairs sit in my office, used only for my twice-weekly production meetings with the staff. He pulled a chair closer to my desk and sat. He crossed one leg over the other and cleared his throat.

"Thank you, Ms. Felix."

I couldn't quite place his accent, but then I'm not very good at that. Not quite Irish. Scottish, maybe, but that didn't seem quite right either.

"What can I do for you, Mr. Quillen?"

"For starters, you can call me Jake," he said. He smiled, maybe trying to be charming. Sadly, he ended up looking peculiar.

"Okay, Jake. I'm Janet."

His smile appeared to be stuck on his face. I waited a moment and it slowly dissolved. After the silence had started to become uncomfortable, he spoke again.

"I have a printing job for you."

"That's what we do." I nodded.

Jacobus Quillen looked uncomfortable. He didn't know if I was joking. I wasn't, but maybe I was being a bit glib. He'd been clutching the satchel close to his chest since he sat down. Now he opened it, paused, looked at me a moment, then returned his attention to the bag. He pulled out a sheaf of papers bound together with twine.

"I have written a book," he said. "A small book," he added, eyes downcast, almost apologetically. I waited until he looked back up at me. "I need it printed."

"Of course."

I expected him to hand the papers, his book, to me. But he didn't.

"It's a very special book," he said.

"We'll take the utmost care with it, Mr. Quil—Jake. How many copies do you need?"

I could see the wheels turning behind his eyes. He hadn't anticipated that question, oddly enough.

"I think two dozen should be sufficient," he said matter-of-factly after a moment.

"Twenty-four copies, no problem." A small job, vanity press. We did similar jobs every so often. Easy enough. I reached across the desk, held my hand out for the papers. He remained reluctant to pass over his manuscript.

"I came to you, Ms. Felix, because I have heard good things about your company." Apparently, he'd decided to ignore my reciprocal request to address me by my first name.

"Thank you." I smiled my customer-friendly smile at him.

"You accommodate specialty requests."

"Certainly." I withdrew my hand; it was starting to feel awkward hovering in mid-air. When it became apparent that he wasn't going to continue, I asked, "What special requests can we accommodate for you?"

He hesitated a moment before answering. "I have my own paper that I need you to use to print the book."

"Okay," I said. I tried to think of a similar request I'd dealt with in my thirteen years running my own print shop. I couldn't come up with one off the top of my head.

"And," he continued slowly, pausing slightly between each word, as though each one deserved a special emphasis, "I need any unused paper returned to me. Any scraps or edges that are trimmed off, as well. Every piece must be returned."

"Of course," I smiled at him. "Shall we discuss size, binding, cover options?"

Slowly, ever so slowly, he lifted the manuscript and extended it in my direction. I intended simply to set it on my desk while I finalized details with Quillen. But when I made contact with the paper, a tingling sensation ran up my arm. My hand felt numb, as though it had fallen asleep suddenly. I felt disoriented.

"Miss Felix."

I looked up. Quillen had had to raise his voice to gain my attention. I realized that he had repeated my name but wasn't sure how many times. I set the manuscript on my desk and my head cleared. "Sorry," I mumbled.

"Quite all right." A sly smile played about Jacobus Quillen's lips.

I showed him samples of other work we had done over the years that I keep in my office for just such a purpose. He decided on a 6"x 9" format, an 80# cover stock, and thermal binding. He promised delivery of the paper on the following day, and I escorted him back to the reception area.

For the rest of the day, I flitted from one minor crisis to the next, like I did most days. It was nearly six o'clock before I returned to my office. Jacobus Quillen's manuscript sat where I had left it on my desk that afternoon. I slipped my jacket on and paused, looking down at the nondescript bundle of papers that sat on one corner of my cluttered workspace. I reached down and ran my fingertips lightly across the manuscript. Once again, I experienced a slight tingling sensation, although it didn't affect me quite as strongly as before. The top page was blank. I peeled back a couple of pages to see what lay underneath. Quillen's manuscript was handwritten in an elaborate calligraphic style that astonished me. A sudden image came to me of Quillen slouched over a desk holding a quill pen dipped in India ink. If all 40 or 50 pages of the manuscript—I hadn't counted or bothered to ask, but I could judge pretty accurately at a glance—were written in the same style, it must have taken him months just to make this one copy. I didn't intend to read the book—it wasn't necessary; my task amounted only to printing copies—I simply admired the style and dedication that went into producing it.

I was still looking at the first page when the loud noise of a slamming door suddenly claimed my attention. Startled, I looked up and out my office door. Nothing moved, no one appeared from the shadows. Faint voices from outside the window indicated that what I'd heard was the banging of the main door downstairs as the last of my first shift employees left the building. I realized that I still held Quillen's manuscript in my hands. My left hand caressed the twine that bound the pages together. It was fine, exquisitely made, but it didn't affect me the way the paper did. Shaking my head, I gently placed the manuscript back on my desk and left the office.

That night I had a strange dream. I remembered very little of it when I woke, except for one scene where I walked outside in a field of gently waving grain. The sky was a deep, peaceful blue; beautiful white cumulus clouds floated through it. The sun shone brightly. A strange little man jumped through the field, taunting me. He appeared as a cross between the Lucky Charms leprechaun and Jacobus Quillen. I didn't remember any more, but I woke up feeling anxious and exhausted.

The box of paper arrived the following day. About two o'clock that afternoon, as I sat in my office looking over some invoices and reports, Amy told me that there was a box with my name on it, marked urgent, down on the loading dock, and that Dave, the shipping supervisor, was anxious to get it out of his area. I walked down to the loading dock, where I asked Dave about it.

He grunted "Over there" and pointed to a small box sitting by itself in one corner of the dock. It couldn't possibly have been in his way, and even if it had been, he could easily have moved it. But I had worked with Dave for almost a decade now and I was acutely aware of his little idiosyncrasies. Best just to humor him. I muttered a barely audible "thanks" and walked over to the box.

I drew a quick, sharp breath when I saw the box up close. My name and the name of my company appeared above the address on a handwritten label affixed to the top. The lettering was in the same calligraphic style as Jacobus Quillen's manuscript. In the box's upper left corner, where one might have included a return address, appeared the single word "Quillen" in that same elaborate script. I stared at it for an inordinately long time, then bent down and traced the Q with my fingertip. Though I couldn't have explained why, I felt positively giddy.

"What is it?"

I glanced up. Dave was standing over me, looking down at me and the box curiously.

"Oh, nothing," I said, hefting the box in my arms as I stood up. I've worked in the printing business most of my adult life and owned my own shop for thirteen years. I know how much various quantities of paper weigh and I knew how heavy this box should be if it were filled with paper, which I had assumed it was. It was remarkably light, and I wondered if I was mistaken as to its contents. It felt like lifting an empty box. I walked away from a bemused looking Dave and returned to my office, the box securely tucked under one arm.

I set the box on the table in my office and picked up a razor box cutter from my desk. As I looked down at the box, I hesitated, the instrument of destruction clutched in my hand. I ran my left hand across the top of the package. It appeared to be ordinary cardboard, sealed with ordinary packing tape. I placed the box cutter along the edge and started to make an incision but stopped after about an inch. Carefully I cut around the label which contained my name and gently removed it. I set that on my desk. I glanced out the open door of my office, glad to see no one looking in. I didn't think I could explain my actions at that moment.

I walked back over to the box. I took a deep breath and sliced along the edges and across the top, opening it fully. Packed carefully inside was Quillen's special paper. It looked like two reams worth or about 1,000 sheets. Probably enough for twenty-four copies of his 40- or so page manuscript, but without much to spare. I reached in and ran my fingers gently over the top sheet. The tingling sensation I'd felt on holding Quillen's manuscript the day before returned, magnified tenfold. My knees shook and I immediately pulled out a chair and sat down. I was breathing heavily.

I realized then that this was one job that I would not just oversee, but that I would take a very hands on approach. I would print Jacobus Quillen's book myself. Which I did over the next couple of days. My lead press operator Charlie was a bit upset when I took over his press and assigned him some busy work to keep him out of my hair. He didn't understand why I couldn't use one of the simpler copiers if I was just making copies of the manuscript. Those copiers could be fed the special paper that Quillen had provided me. I couldn't explain it to Charlie—I'm not sure I could explain it sufficiently to myself—so I didn't even try. I used my status as boss and owner of the company to dismiss his questions out of hand. I shifted other, waiting jobs to the back burner.

I carefully printed copies of each page one at a time until I had a completed book. I trimmed the edges of the pages to the proper size and collected each piece of scrap. These I placed into a separate, unmarked cardboard box which I stored surreptitiously in my office. I placed each completed copy of Quillen's manuscript on a shelf behind my desk where no one was likely to notice or touch them. Once done with one, I repeated the process. It would have been quicker to make multiple copies of each page and collate them, but I chose not to. I was in no hurry; Quillen had not given me a deadline, and I wanted to savor the process.

Many of my employees looked at me askance during the days I worked on Jacobus Quillen's book. I was unavailable, unable to answer questions, resolve disputes, settle arguments, or make sure things ran smoothly, which was my usual mode of operation. I was lost in my own little world. Contact with Quillen's paper sent tingles along my skin with each touch. After time spent making one copy of his manuscript, I somehow felt both energized and exhausted. I often closed my office door and sat behind my desk with my eyes closed for long minutes before returning to the floor to make the next copy.

By the end of the third day, two dozen copies of Quillen's manuscript sat piled on the shelf. I had used every sheet of paper that Quillen had provided. The book was 42 pages long, so 24 copies took 1008 pieces of paper. He had apparently counted it out to the last sheet. I wondered what he would have done if I'd made a mistake and had to re-copy even a single page. Surprisingly, I hadn't. The scrap box of trimmed edges sat underneath the table in my office. Whenever I ran a hand along one of the manuscript copies, the tingling sensation started along my fingertips and palm and ran up my arm. If I stood with my hands placed atop two manuscripts (and I did this several times, I admit), the sensation would spread across my shoulders, down my back, wrap around my ribcage to my stomach, finally creeping slowly down my thighs. By the time it reached my knees, I could no longer remain standing. My entire body felt numb, but the sensation was amazingly pleasant. Once during college, I volunteered for a psychological experiment in order to make a little extra money. I was immersed in a sensory deprivation tank for half an hour. It had been the most intense experience of my life. Not only did I feel like I was floating in space, in a void, with no light and no sound, but my mind was at peace like no other time in my life. I felt content. Serene. I'd never felt anything close to that sensation again. Until Jacobus Quillen's paper came into my office. The feeling now was similar, but even more intense.

I checked the schedule and found that the thermal binding machine was free for the next several days. It wouldn't take long to bind 24 copies of the manuscript. Quillen had requested a plain, dark blue cover on 80# stock and that it be left blank. I didn't think anything unusual of it at the time—he had made the request the first day we met in my office—but now I began to wonder why he hadn't had a title for his book. Perhaps he wanted to add the title later in that same calligraphic script. It was an idle thought. I felt little desire to read Quillen's manuscript. It was none of my particular business, after all, and despite my actions of the last few days, I was a professional. Moreover, if I searched my feelings, I realized that whatever was in the manuscript, I knew it couldn't compare to the feelings brought about by the paper itself.

Once the books were covered and bound, I reluctantly placed them in a box—with all the delicacy one might use when handling fine crystal—and sealed it. I set the box in a corner of my office where no one would question its presence, if indeed, anyone even noticed it. I sat behind my desk, my elbows resting on top, and my face propped in my open hands. I was exhausted. I hadn't slept much the night before; I'd anticipated binding the manuscripts and knew that once they were boxed up, I wouldn't have the opportunity to touch them again, making contact, skin on paper. I'd tossed and turned in bed, awake at 3:00 a.m., failing to fall back asleep.

Now I looked up, noticing the box of paper scraps—the trimmed edges from Quillen's manuscript—underneath the table. I walked over to it, somewhat unsteady on my feet. I pulled out the one chair that sat in front of the box. It was accessible. I only had to kneel down and I could reach the box—reach into the box.

The intercom buzzed. Amy's voice—harsh and electronic—filled the room. It startled me. "Janet, that Jacob Quillen guy is on line one. What's the status of his job? You were working on that yourself, right?"

"Jacobus Quillen," I corrected her absentmindedly.

"What?"

"Nothing." I shook my head, attempting to clear the cobwebs. "It's finished. Tell him it's ready to ship out."

"Will do."

The buzzing of the intercom ceased when Amy disconnected. I looked around the room. Thirteen years I had spent in this corner office. Today it looked foreign to me. Why was I so disoriented? Jacobus Quillen had called? Why did it seem odd to me to think of him using a phone? This was 2010. Of course he used the phone. I sprinted to my office door and pulled it open. Amy looked up at me from her desk, surprised. I was out of breath. I could only imagine what I looked like. I noticed the phone's receiver sat cradled on her desk.

"Quillen?" I managed to say.

Amy nodded. "He said he'd pick up the order himself tomorrow," she said. "That's okay, isn't it? We don't have to ship it," she added, probably concerned by the state I was in.

"Fine," I said softly. "I just wanted to talk to him."

She shrugged. "He'll be here tomorrow. You can see him then."

"Of course."

"Unless you want me to call him back." Her hand hovered over the phone.

"No, no, tomorrow's fine."

I turned back into my office, shutting the door behind me. I leaned back against it, eyes closed. Deep breaths, I told myself, counting them. Eight, ten, twelve. I felt calm. When I opened my eyes, my gaze fell on the box of paper scraps underneath the desk, the chair pulled out next to it. I walked over to it, knelt down, and pulled out the box until it touched my knees. I took another deep breath, held it, then plunged my hands into the box. The sensation was ecstatic.

The next day I came to work tired and grumpy. I hadn't slept much during the night (again!) and what little sleep I did manage was filled with strange and disturbing dreams, the content of which fled rapidly upon awakening, but they left me feeling drained and uneasy. I was short with my employees—I might have made one of them, a college student who worked part-time, cry when I yelled at her for five minutes for repeatedly showing up late—and I hid out in my office from mid-morning on. I ate my lunch in silence, staring at the box of paper scraps underneath the table. Shortly before two p.m., Amy buzzed me on the intercom. She had wisely left me alone until then.

"Jacob, uh, Jacobus Quillen is here to see you," she said.

"Send him in."

The door opened and he entered, looking much the same as he had the first time, the only previous time I'd seen him. He wore the same tweed jacket with his tweed cap tucked under one arm. He extended a hand, somewhat shyly it seemed. His grip was surprisingly firm when we shook. "Ms. Felix," he said softly, "a pleasure to see you once again."

"And you, Mr. Quillen."

"Jake," he smiled.

"Jake," I acknowledged.

We both stood in front of my desk—I'd come around to meet him—and after a few moments of awkward silence, Quillen cleared his throat.

"So," he said, "my book?"

My eyes went to the box of finished and bound manuscripts on the shelf. Quillen looked at me without speaking. "Of course," I said, and retrieved the box, setting it on the table. He rested one hand on the box, and a small smile flickered across his features. Then he looked back up at me, again without speaking. I couldn't remember feeling quite this uncomfortable with a client before. A moment passed before I realized what he wanted.

"Excuse me," I said, edging past him. I picked up the box of paper scraps from under the table and set it on top next to the other box. He opened one of the top flaps and glanced inside. Then he closed it and looked back at me.

"Very good," he said, finally.

"Jake," I stammered. "I have to ask. The paper …?"

"Ah," he said, and a broad grin broke over his face for a moment before he brought it under control. "I guessed that someone of your knowledge and expertise might have noticed."

"Noticed?"

He smiled but said nothing.

"Where does it come from?" I asked.

"A special creation. My people have known the secret for generations."

I nodded, though I wasn't sure I understood. His people?

"Where are you from?" I blurted out.

He shook his head and smiled wistfully. "The old country is long gone," he whispered. A long moment passed in silence, and I realized that he wasn't going to say anything else. I wasn't going to learn anything more about Jacobus Quillen or the mysterious box of paper that he'd brought into my life. But I also knew that I couldn't let this go.

"Mr. Quillen—Jake, I wonder if we might discuss an alternative to our contract?"

He waited for me to continue.

"Rather than the payment we agreed upon," I ventured, my words tumbling out quickly, "might I have more of your paper?"

He just smiled.

"Another box?" I asked. "One more box. The same as before."

Throughout my life, my career, I have dealt with many, many customers. Some were difficult, even impossible, to please under any circumstances. Sometimes they were dissatisfied with the quality of our work. Some were easy to deal with, a relief. Most were content with the services we provided. The look on Jacobus Quillen's face at that moment could only be interpreted as one of complete satisfaction.

"That is acceptable," was all that he said.

Quillen lifted both boxes in his arms, the scraps of paper atop the completed manuscripts. I offered to help, but he refused. The boxes appeared to weigh nothing to him, much as the original had to me. His tweed cap back on his head, he looked like a picture of unparalleled quaintness.

The box of paper requested arrived the next day. Looking inside, I guessed it contained two reams. A faint brush of my hand on the top sheet told me that it was the same type of paper as I'd used to print Quillen's book.

I have not seen nor heard from Jacobus Quillen since. The box of special paper sits in the corner of my office, behind my desk, where no one else should give it a second glance. Nevertheless, I keep it sealed and have a plant sitting on top of it. Some days I move the plant aside, open the box, and simply look inside. Some days I reach in and touch the top sheet of paper. It still sends a shiver through me.

I will ration the use of this paper, as though it were the most precious in the world. It might be. I've used only two sheets since the box was delivered to me. On the first I wrote a thank you letter to Jacobus Quillen. That letter sits in the middle drawer of my desk. I have no idea where to send it, or how. On the second I wrote, using an antique fountain pen, a love letter to my longtime boyfriend. I brought it to his house one evening and handed it to him personally, then sat and watched while he read it. The night that followed was one of the most amazing of my life.

8. Bones

The first time I see the Kid is off in the woods one night on my way home. His eyes, barely visible under a shaggy mop of dirty blond hair, lock with mine as I drive past. He wears a plaid shirt with a dark green pattern and dark jeans. He's young, not more than a teenager. Something white dangles from his right hand, but I'm past him before I can tell what it is. He stands stock still, watches me pass, turns his head just enough to keep his gaze locked on my truck.

I wonder where he came from, his presence here unexpected. But I don't dwell on it. It's been an especially long day, I'm tired, exhausted, and look forward to nothing more than a long soak in my makeshift bathtub. I consider myself lucky. I live in a cabin in the woods, miles away from my nearest neighbors. I've got running water. Most days, I get electricity for a couple of hours in the evening. Considering the state of the economy and the way that most other people in these hills live since the events they call simply "The Disaster," I am lucky indeed. I've even got a job—making deliveries—and my own truck. Better than most.

When I get to my cabin, I climb out of the truck and make my way slowly to the back of the house. I'm limping a bit due to the injury I suffered in my left leg a few months back. Most of the time, it doesn't bother me anymore, but like I said, it's been a long day. Sitting in that truck for long stretches doesn't do the leg any good. I lean against a corner of the cabin, and let go with two long, low whistles. After a couple of minutes, I hear a rustling noise in the woods. Suddenly, my Jack Russell terrier, Wendell, comes bounding down the slope. I let him roam the hills when I'm off at work. He jumps up on my legs and I rub his head and back. His tail wags furiously. We walk back to the front door of the cabin. I unlock both padlocks and we go in. I'm disappointed to see the electricity level is so low tonight that my lamps barely glow. No bath tonight, but I'm too tired to care much. I dump some food in Wendell's bowl—who knows what he managed to find in the woods today—and peel off my clothes. I stumble into the bedroom, lie down, and fall asleep in moments.

The next day when I approach the spot I saw him, memories of the Kid resurface. This access road I drive down every day is seldom used—one of the things I appreciate most about my little cabin in the woods. No one is likely to come upon me by accident. I don't get company. A couple hundred yards before I get to the spot where I'd seen the Kid, I notice a rusted-out car sitting on the side of the road. I'd seen it here yesterday but guess I was so tired I ignored it. I drive a bit farther, past the Kid's spot— yesterday he'd been off the road, under the trees, in the shadows—when I see him again. Today he's walking along the side of the road, where the cracked blacktop meets the dirt and grass of the fields. He's coming toward me, walking back toward the rusty car. I figure it must be his, a home base maybe. He probably lives in it. I ease my foot off the accelerator as soon as I see him, and coast slowly past.

He keeps his eyes on his feet, doesn't even look up this time as I cruise past. He carries a large white pail—the kind of industrial bucket that restaurants used in the pre-Disaster days. The pail is overflowing with some kind of white objects, jammed in there haphazardly. The setting sun shines through the dappled leaves of the trees on either side of the roadway and reflects brightly off the white pail. It's not until I'm past him that I realize that the pail's full of bones. Bones that are too white, too regularly sized, to be real. Not animal bones, then. Fake bones.

I'm pleased to see the lights in the cabin burn brighter tonight. The electric current is stronger. Once in the cabin, I draw myself a bath. I've got an old ceramic, claw-footed bathtub that I scavenged several years ago. I enjoy a hot bath a few times a week. I rigged up a set of hoses that run through a series of old metal and plastic containers in a way that heats the water. It's an ingenious, elaborate set-up, and I'm not about to share my secret. Like I said, I'm lucky. As I ease into the hot water, Wendell lying on the floor beside me happily gnawing a bone he brought back from the woods today, I wonder about the Kid.

While it's not completely unheard of, it's definitely rare to see strangers in this area. And there's a look about him, something I've seen before, that makes me think he belongs around here. But I've never seen him before, I'm sure of that. My nearest "neighbors" live miles away, and the Kid is uncomfortably close to my home. What is he doing in the woods? And what's with that bucket of bones? The question swirls through my mind for a moment, then I just let the warmth of the water, the feel of the liquid surrounding me, and the rhythmic sounds of Wendell's chewing slowly drain all conscious thought from my mind.

When I drive home the next day, I'm anxious to see if the Kid will be out here again. The broken down, rusty car sits in the same spot. The Kid definitely lives in the car. Then I spot him, just a few feet from where I saw him the last couple of days. He sits on a mound of freshly turned dirt, maybe eight feet from the road's edge. The same green plaid shirt and dark jeans—probably the only clothes he owns. His brown work boots—I didn't notice them before—are dirty, scuffed, and full of holes. It's a wonder they stay on his feet. Like the Kid himself, his outfit has seen better days. Then again, haven't we all?

The pile of newly dug dirt he sits on is a deep, rich brown. His white bucket lies nearby, and he reaches into it while I cruise slowly past. He looks my way but ignores me and returns to his task. He's burying bones in the dirt.

I drive on, but it all makes me wonder: what is the Kid up to? Suddenly I think—though I have no idea why—that maybe he's trying to create a fake dinosaur, planting the bones, hoping they'll be discovered. But why? If it's a scam, I can't figure it out. Are there any archeological sites nearby? Somehow that sounds familiar, but I can't quite remember why. It's there in my mind, but it's distant, like trying to remember the name of the state where we live. Back when there were still states, I mean.

After parking the truck at my cabin, I sneak back until I can see the Kid. I creep slowly through the woods, and an hour probably passes. But the Kid's still in the same place, sitting on the pile of fresh dirt, not moving. I crouch among the trees and underbrush, still, silent, barely breathing, as I watch him. He rests, his breathing hard but steady. After a minute, he gets up, then walks over to a nearby tree and sits again, resting his back against the tree. I circle around, crawling ever so slowly along the forest floor, careful not to make a sound, until I'm behind the Kid. I said I'm lucky, and my luck holds. Autumn hasn't yet arrived completely, and the ground is damp and spongy, not covered with dry, brittle leaves that would make it harder to stay silent.

I can't figure out what the Kid's up to, but I do know it's foolish, maybe even illegal. So what I do next is a favor to the Kid. I crawl on my stomach, inching closer to the mound of dirt and bucket of bones. When I'm close enough to reach the bucket, I pause and lie still for a very long time. The Kid doesn't move. His head rests on his chest. I think I hear him snore. Slowly I stand up, the bucket in my right hand. The Kid still doesn't move. I head off along the road, back toward my cabin. My leg aches. If I'd stopped when I drove by earlier, this would have been a lot easier. Driving instead of walking, I mean. Of course, getting the bucket away from the Kid might have been difficult.

As I walk along, my mood brightens. The angle of the sunlight through the trees makes me happy. Occasionally I hear a squirrel running along the branches or the chirp of birds, but for the most part, the wood is quiet. The bucket feels light and pleasant. I start to swing it back and forth as I walk.

"Hey!"

The voice comes from behind me. I turn and I see the Kid. He's followed me, no doubt wants his stuff back. I am still a fair distance ahead of him. His shout came too soon, letting me know he's there. Unless he doesn't care. I start to run.

As I sprint along, I can hear his footsteps behind me getting closer. Glancing over my shoulder, I see him gaining on me. It won't take him long to catch up. Much as I might like to deny it, I'm an old man, and he's just a kid. I know he's going to catch up to me soon. Without breaking stride, I toss the bucket of bones off to my right, as far as I can fling it. I'm breathing heavily, and I feel a sharp twinge in my side. My legs feel like lead, the left one aches, that damn injury again.

Assuming the Kid stopped to get his bucket, I figure I've put enough distance between us by now. I stop running, lean forward, my hands on my thighs. I cough, hawk up some phlegm and spit. I wipe my mouth and stand up straight. When I turn, the Kid is standing no more than twenty feet away. He stands still, staring at me. He doesn't even look like he's breathing hard. Damn him.

"Look," I say, trying to catch my breath. "I'm trying to help you out, okay? I don't know exactly what you're planning, but it won't work."

The Kid just stares at me, that mop of blond hair hanging over his eyes. Now I can see he is breathing hard. That makes me feel a little better, more confident. "Hey," I say, "can I just have one of those bones?" I don't know why I ask him that, but I suddenly feel an overwhelming desire. I need one of those bones.

He crouches down, digging through the dirt at his feet. I watch him carefully. Suddenly he flings an arm toward me, tosses something at me. I reach up with my right hand and grab it. The Kid made a good throw; I don't even have to move to catch it, just bring my hand up near my shoulder. I look at what's in my hand. It's white, about eight inches long, but flat. Two horn-like projections on each end. It's an old wrench, abandoned, bleached white over the years. He must have picked it up out of the dirt.

I look over at the Kid and smile. "Nice, kid, a wrench." It's all there is to say. I toss it back to him and turn to leave. I don't bother to watch to see if he catches it.

I take a couple of steps away, and he yells something. It might be a word; I can't tell. I turn around. The Kid hasn't moved from where he stood, but now he holds a piece of wood. About four feet long, flat, rounded corners. An old skateboard, maybe? If it is, it's cracked and missing its wheels. I didn't see it before and now I wonder where it came from. Is there a junkyard, a dump, somewhere around here? Maybe he's had it in his car all along. The way he's holding it—crosswise in front of him—makes it look like a weapon.

"I won't hurt you," I tell him. "I don't want to fight."

"I won't hurt you either."

It's the first time I've heard him say more than one word. His voice is soft, mellifluous, almost musical. But I don't know if I believe him. I'm sure he can read that in my face. He's got no expression. Even when he confronted me after chasing me down, he didn't look angry.

Suddenly, without speaking or looking away from me, he throws the board off to his right, one-handed. It ricochets off a nearby tree trunk and heads straight for my head. I duck just in time to avoid being beaned. How did he do that? And he doesn't want to hurt me? Really?

"Liar," I say. "Is that the kind of bones you got there, Kid? Liar-saurus?" I don't know where that comes from.

I keep my eyes on the Kid for a moment longer. A change comes over his face, a look I'm not sure I can describe. Thoughtful, maybe? Regret? Resignation? Anyway, after a minute, the Kid turns and walks back the way he came from. I walk the other way.

The next night, driving home, I notice the rusted old car is gone. I can't believe the Kid got it running. Maybe someone towed it away for parts. I've got no idea. I stop next to the dirt mound, leave the truck running while I climb down and walk over to it. The dirt's been spread around some. I kick at it, getting dust and dirt all over my boots and the lower half of my pants. I don't uncover any bones.

When I get to the cabin, I see something sitting in front of the door. Bright white, about fifteen inches long, made out of some kind of hard plastic. One of the Kid's fake bones. I smile as I pick it up. It's heavier than it looks. I poke around the area around the cabin, but I don't see the Kid or any other sign he's been here. I don't expect to. Wendell is very excited when he sees the bone, but I don't give it to him. I set it on a special shelf in my cabin. It's not a bone for my dog. It was left here for me.

9. (No) Qualms

Midafternoon. The bar was nearly empty. A young bartender, looking bored, dragged a rag along the counter wiping up imaginary spills. She looked to be about twenty, and I absently wondered if she might be a student at the local college. She reminded me of myself at that age. An old man sat at the oval-shaped bar in the center of the room, mumbling to himself and drinking glass after glass of cheap tap beer. Two young women sat at a table under the front window. They drank colorful concoctions from tall glasses, talking quietly and occasionally erupting into embarrassed laughter.

I sat alone in a booth at the very back of the room, trying to hide in the darkness. I realized that I was fidgeting with my wedding band, turning it around and around. I reached for my Diet Coke. Most of the ice had melted. Why had I come here so early? Why had I come here at all?

A couple of afternoons a week, I worked for a small company, doing data input, more to get out of the house than anything else, really. I loved my kids more than anything, but spending my entire day, day after day, with two preschoolers was starting to drive me over the edge. I needed some adult conversation. My few hours of work barely paid for the kids' daycare, but it saved my sanity. My husband Jim was very supportive of me working. That was Jim: quiet, sweet, understanding. I loved my husband, so what was I doing here?

I met David a few months ago at work. We exchanged a few hellos around the office before he sat down across from me in the break room one afternoon and introduced himself. Immediately, I found him easier to talk to than anyone else at work. He seemed to know instinctively what was on my mind. He listened patiently, smiling, while I spilled out endless stories about my kids, Jason and Lisa. I was positive

I was boring him. Our talk soon moved on to current events, history, books. He was extremely well read and knowledgeable, and unafraid to voice his opinions. For the next few weeks, David seemed to appear every time I sat down for my 15-minute break. I started looking forward to work, and those breaks, more than ever. I saw David at other times during the afternoon, but those breaks were ours.

Most of the others in the office were political conservatives. We lived in a very conservative city. I'd kept my more liberal views to myself but I found a like-minded soul in David, who was, if anything, more liberal than I. Though he was often referred to as "our token liberal," David's other charms didn't go unnoticed by the women in the office. He was tall, lean, and dark, the perfect mysterious stranger. But he was soft-spoken, kept to himself most of the time, and I felt privileged, special, when I saw his more passionate side during our talks.

David reminded me of Jim, or more accurately, the Jim I had met during college: passionate and exciting. Five years of marriage had mellowed Jim. His job distracted him; he had gained twenty pounds. But he was so good with the children. I had no reason to complain. I certainly didn't look the same as I did in college. I noticed dark circles under my eyes most of the time. I took to dressing in bulky sweatshirts and cropped my hair short. I tried to look less feminine, to match the way I felt.

I remember the first time David touched me. I was sitting at my desk when he appeared behind me. He leaned over, resting a hand on my shoulder, while he made some little joke about the file I was working on. I don't remember if I even replied; all I recall is the tingling sensation of my skin where he placed his hand. After that, I watched every movement of those hands, strong yet tender, sighing under my breath with warm pleasure when he'd place one on the small of my back guiding me out of the break room, back to my lonely desk. David started walking me to my car after work, sometimes we'd talk for long minutes before I reluctantly excused myself to pick up the kids from daycare. I relished the attention he gave me.

A week ago, after his usual "see you Thursday," he leaned forward and kissed me on the cheek. He pulled back quickly, looking shocked, and stammered "I'm sorry." I smiled. His dark eyes showed genuine concern. "It's all right," I told him, patting his arm reassuringly. My knees felt weak as I got in the car. I don't think I stopped shaking until I got home.

The front door to the bar opened, briefly flooding the gloom with afternoon sunlight, and David walked in. The two young women at the front whispered furtively, glancing at him, and I felt a twinge of undeserved jealousy. David smiled when he saw me. He sat down without preamble, said "Hello."

"I'm not sure I should be here," I blurted out. He looked confused and a little hurt for a second, and I immediately regretted saying it.

"You don't have to be," he said, smiling.

"I'm ... I want to be. I'm okay. Just nervous." I giggled. God, I sounded like a schoolgirl. Grade school.

"Any trouble getting out?" he asked.

I might have felt insulted then, used. But there was such sympathy in his voice, I knew he was concerned about me. I shook my head. "Jim thinks I'm picking up an extra few hours at work."

I could have asked him how he got away from work, but I didn't. I wanted to talk about anything else. Thankfully, the bartender, doubling as waitress, appeared at the table just then. "What can I get you?" she asked. I looked up. Her eyes sparkled as they focused on David, as though she was offering him something more than just a drink order. What was it about him? I looked at him and felt that familiar weakness in my knees. If I'd been standing, I would have collapsed right then. He had a power to him.

He smiled casually at the waitress. "I'll have a Blue Moon, if you have it."

"We do." She turned to me. "Another Diet Coke?" she asked, her voice verging on contempt.

"I'll take a Blue Moon, too," I volunteered, wondering where my sudden courage had come from. I felt threatened by her and protective of David. Her eyebrows arched slightly, but she turned away silently.

David was smiling. "I thought you didn't drink," he said, with the barest nod of his head toward my half-empty glass of Diet Coke.

"I didn't say that." I smiled at him, feeling more comfortable by the moment. "I said I'd never been drunk."

The waitress returned with two glasses and two bottles, which David poured for both of us. He raised his glass in a silent toast. God, how his eyes shone in this darkened corner, as though they were lit from within instead of reflecting light. My throat had gone dry, and I took a long drink. The beer tasted wonderful. "Although," I added, licking foam from my lips, "it's been years."

We exchanged some small talk, recent conversations with co-workers, current political events. I'm sure I told inane stories about my kids. How could any man want me when I told stories about my children? But I sensed that he did want me. More than that, I knew it. I could see it in his eyes. How long had it been, how many years since I'd seen a look like that?

I can't remember him saying much about his past, and I didn't press. There were rumors at work, of course: there had been a nasty divorce, or that he was widowed, or even that he was gay "A single guy who looks that great," Amy had whispered one day. "He's got to be gay. Too bad, too." Amy had a boyfriend at home, but it didn't matter to me. I knew what I wanted to know about him.

I babbled on about myself. I played basketball in college; we were state champions my junior year. I had a brother in

Washington, D.C., who worked for a Senator. I hadn't dated much before Jim; we'd met during my last semester of college. I worked for a public research firm for two years until Jason was born. Jim and I agreed that I would stay home and take care of the children. No, I didn't regret that, but sometimes I felt that my life had been placed on hold, that I was missing out on something. I had always been a good kid; my dad was a Presbyterian minister. I'd never tried drugs, never even been drunk.

I'd never been unfaithful to my husband.

"I'm glad you agreed," he said quietly. "To meet me," he added after a slight pause.

I blushed, looked down at my glass.

"Not having second thoughts, are you?" he asked. "Qualms?"

"No," I lied, afraid to meet his eyes. What would happen, what would he do, if he knew how scared I truly was? "No qualms."

"I've been flirting with you for weeks now," he admitted, his voice light, but serious, and full of life. "Surely you know that."

I looked up, shocked. Two minutes ago, I could have easily, truthfully denied it. Now I saw it all plainly. He had been flirting with me from the beginning. I must have been blind not to see it. I could hardly believe it.

David reached out, placed a hand on top of mine. I felt flushed. My hand, under his, seemed to be on fire. The warmth traveled up my arm, across my shoulders, down my back. I took a deep breath, vividly conscious of the swelling of my breasts. The sensation of heat filled my stomach for a moment, then flowed into and between my thighs. I closed my eyes.

David removed his hand. I opened my eyes and saw him watching me over the rim of his glass as he drank. I reached for my beer and drained most of what was left.

We sat in silence for a while. His eyes seemed almost to glow in the darkness when he looked into mine. He wore a twill button-down shirt with the top couple of buttons undone. I noticed a small brush of dark chest hair underneath. The rest of the bar, the rest of the world, faded into the background. He and I, this scratched Formica table between us, were the only things that existed in the universe. How long we sat there like that, I don't know. Worlds may have been born, lived, and died. It might have been a few seconds.

He reached out a hand to mine again. The warmth returned, but softer this time, more controlled, like stepping into a heated pool on a warm summer's day. "Do you want to go?" he asked, his voice barely a whisper.

I nodded. I don't think I could have spoken.

He paid for our drinks as I stood demurely behind him, trying again to hide. I felt awkward and nervous. I didn't want to be recognized. This was irrational, I told myself; no one here would know me. Outside, the bright sunlight brought me back to the world. David looked up the street, one hand shading his eyes. "I parked right next to you," he said casually. I walked close to him as we headed up the street, aware of each time my arm brushed his. We stopped next to my car. "Why don't you follow me?" he suggested. He took my hand, gently squeezed it, smiled, and winked.

I followed him without thinking. I donned my sunglasses to drive, shifted when I needed, braked when I needed, turned where he turned, but I was on automatic. I could have been asleep.

David turned into the parking garage of a downtown hotel. I knew its reputation for quality, probably the most expensive hotel in town. He was waiting beside my car when I got out. Smiling, he leaned toward me, softly kissed my lips. It was the first time he'd kissed me since that afternoon in the parking lot after work. It lasted maybe two seconds. When he straightened, I moved forward, not wanting to lose contact with his lips. I stood on my toes, my face inches from his shining eyes. I slowly rocked back unto my heels. Hand-in-hand we walked to the hotel entrance.

The girl behind the desk smiled as we approached. She was perky, all smiles, her blond hair tied back in a ponytail. She might have been eighteen. "May I help you?" she asked behind perfect white teeth.

"I have a reservation," David told her, handing her a credit card.

She reluctantly tore her eyes away from David to look down at her ledger. My David, I thought happily, absurdly. I gave his hand a squeeze and he smiled at me.

"There you are, Mr. Parker," the desk clerk said, handing back his credit card. As David signed the slip, the girl looked briefly at me. Her eyes seemed to say, "lucky you." She looked back at David before she saw me smile in agreement. "Room 702."

David thanked her as he took the key and we headed for the elevators. "Reservations?" I asked. "You're awfully sure of yourself." He squeezed my hand slightly but didn't reply.

The room approached elegance. No vacation I'd ever been on had I ever stayed anywhere close to this. David tossed the key on a table and walked to the window. I glanced at the king size bed, decided to sit on the sofa. As I sunk onto its plush cushions, my eyes never left David. He stood abnormally still. I wondered if he was watching something. Then he pulled the curtains closed and turned to me. He was dressed simply: blue jeans, athletic shoes, and the twill shirt. Somehow, I thought, he managed to make it look stunning.

I began to feel self-conscious. I wore tennis shoes and jeans myself, and a black, long-sleeved pullover, a bit less bulky than my usual. David had once told me that he liked this shirt. I couldn't remember the last occasion I'd dressed up for and started to wish that I'd dug out a dress or a skirt today.

David sat next to me, one arm around my shoulder. his fingers played with the short hair at the back of my neck. He leaned toward me, kissed me, and I shifted to face him. One hand on his shoulder, my other slid around his waist to the small of his back. His right hand moved up the length of my thigh, then rested on my hip. His lips parted and his tongue tentatively licked my lips. I opened my mouth and with my tongue invited his in.

After kissing me for a few moments, he pulled back. His fingers moved along my neck to my cheek. "I like your earrings," he said softly, as his fingers found my ear lobes. They were plain silver hoops about two inches in diameter. I could barely whisper "Thank you."

"I like your dark eyes," he said, and softly kissed the skin below them. My eyes closed as he drew nearer, and his lips brushed my eyelids.

"I like yours, too," I breathed.

He moved on to my ears, which he kissed softly, then to the side of my neck. If I had any resistance left, any reluctance still (though, truthfully, I'm sure I didn't), it would have vanished at that moment. I grabbed the sides of his head, kissed him forcefully, and pushed him back on the couch until I lay on top of him.

He wiggled out from under me, took my hands in his, and led me over to the bed. We sat on the edge and kissed. I unbuttoned his shirt and slipped it back over his broad shoulders. I breathed faster as I ran a hand through his dark chest hairs. He slipped a hand under my shirt. I'm sure I moaned when he touched my breast. His hands were so light, almost ticklish, on my body. I shivered slightly. He pulled the shirt over my head, and I fell back on the bed, his lips and hands moving over me.

"Just a minute," I whispered, slipping out from under him. He looked curious as I picked up my purse. "Diaphragm," I mouthed, picking it out of my purse, and ducked into the bathroom. When I returned, he had stripped the bed to just a sheet, and wore only his jeans. I had left my shoes in the bathroom but put my jeans back on. I wanted him to undress me as much as I wanted to undress him.

The next hour seemed both to fly by and to last forever. We explored each other's bodies as though the two of us were inventing sex. We tried things I had never experienced, things I had only fantasized about, and things that I had never even imagined. Every new aspect was like being reborn. Never had I felt such pleasure. I was more excited— and more exciting—than I had ever been. Everything seemed new, strange, delightfully forbidden. Everything felt wonderful. It all seemed natural, as though we were meant for this moment and this moment alone. I felt fulfilled in a way I didn't know a person could be fulfilled, down to my very soul. I had no idea where these feelings came from. I felt loved, adored. Worshipped. I couldn't get enough of him. More than once I wondered if we'd both survive the afternoon.

Afterward I lay coiled next to him, one leg over his, an arm flung across his chest. He hugged me close and kissed my forehead. We glistened with the sweet sweat of hard exercise. "That," I started, then bit my lip. David waited. "That was fantastic," I finished limply, knowing words could not express my feelings. I said as much.

David was quiet. He ran one finger in slow circles around my shoulder. Suddenly frightened, I said, "Tell me that this wasn't ... that there's ... that we ..." I couldn't give voice to my fear.

But he understood. He cupped a hand under my chin, gently turning my head until I was looking into his eyes. "I promise you'll see me again," he said slowly, confidently, deliberately. Reassured, I snuggled closer, my head on his chest.

I don't remember falling asleep. When I woke, the afternoon light was more angled, less glaring. Must be getting late, I thought as I stretched. I smiled, feeling satisfied. Slowly I realized that I was alone. I sat up, pulling the sheet close around my body. The hotel room appeared less elegant than it had before. The alarm clock next to the bed flashed 12:00. It must have come unplugged. I wondered what time it actually was. I picked up the phone and dialed the front desk. Six o'clock, I was told. The voice sounded like the young blonde we'd seen earlier.

I got out of bed, the sheet wrapped around my naked torso, and wandered around the room. David was gone, his clothes vanished with him. No trace of him remained. So that's the way it is, I thought, suddenly bitter. I threw the sheet back onto the bed. Then I noticed something lying on the nightstand. I walked over and picked it up. My diaphragm, unused. But I was sure I had put it in earlier. Hadn't I? I ran a hand across my stomach.

I could smell David's scent on me, the smell of sex. I decided to shower though I knew I was already late. Jim would be wondering where I was. My God, Jim. The sudden weight of guilt forced me to sit down on the bed. My eyes filled with tears; one ran down my cheek. No time for this, I told myself. I forced myself to stand and walk to the bathroom.

I felt more composed after I'd showered. Guilt and satisfaction mixed with curiosity about David to form a new, not entirely unpleasant, emotion. I dressed quickly and left the room. The perky blonde at the desk had been replaced by a well-dressed young man who nodded as I walked by. I ignored him.

I was shaking by the time I got home, afraid to see my husband. Jim just smiled when I walked in and made some offhand comment about my having to work late. My laugh was nervous, but he didn't seem to notice. He had fixed dinner for the kids—I nearly burst into tears the moment I saw them—and saved some for me. I tried to eat. The house looked exactly as I had left it. *Why wouldn't it?* Jason wouldn't rest until he'd told me a dozen stories about daycare. Within an hour, I started to feel, well, normal. I would see David the next time I worked, if not before. Though butterflies fluttered in my stomach whenever I thought of his name, his face, his body, I tried to settle down and get back to my regular life, though I knew I had changed that forever.

The next day I worked, David wasn't there. My co-workers related to me the same as always, but I felt too uncomfortable to ask about him. Somehow, I felt they knew our torrid secret. The afternoon passed slowly.

That night I felt lonely and depressed. I went to bed early, as soon as the kids were down. By morning, my mood had swung around to anger. I was irate that he hadn't at least called. Though he'd never phoned me before, things were different now. Weren't they? I deserved something, some contact. When the kids were napping, I picked up the phone and cradled it twice before I finally dialed information. They found no listing for David Parker. I lost control, yelled at the operator, and slammed the phone down. I don't know how long I sat in the kitchen sobbing. When I heard Lisa cry out in her sleep, I got up, wiped my face, and went to check on her.

The following afternoon I went to work again. Again, as I feared, there was no David. When I asked a co-worker about him, pointing to David's desk, she looked confused and told me that she didn't remember anyone sitting there. After a long, lonely break, I stopped by Amy's desk. Amy was the office gossip; if anyone knew where David was, it would be her. "Have you seen David around?" I asked, trying desperately to sound casual, and afraid I'd failed.

"Who?" she asked. I wondered for a second if everyone was playing mind games with me, until deciding that I didn't need to get paranoid.

"You know," I smiled, nodding toward his desk. "David."

She looked quizzically at me.

"David," I repeated. "David Parker? The cute one?"

Amy shook her head. "I don't know who you're talking about. And, believe me, I know all the cute guys," she added, winking.

Numb, I returned to my desk where I sat doing nothing for half an hour or more. Finally, fear and nervousness gave me something close to courage, and I walked up to the Personnel Office. Grey-haired Mrs. Benson smiled at me; her kind eyes sympathetic behind wire rim bifocals. "I don't think there's a David Parker here," she said.

"Are you sure?"

"I'll double check." She punched keys on her computer. I bit down hard on my lower lip. "No," she said, turning back to me. "No David Parker."

"You mean he quit? Can you tell me when he left?" My voice rose.

"No, I mean there's never been a David Parker employed here." I slumped against her desk. "Are you all right, dear?" she asked, reaching out to touch my arm. "You look a little pale."

"I'm all right," I told her, straightening. "I must have the name wrong."

I returned to my desk, collapsed in my chair. I remembered David. He was real. I remembered him working here, I remembered our breaks together, our talks. I remembered his voice, his eyes, his face. I remembered the touch of his hand on my shoulder. I remembered his kiss. I remembered the feel of his body under me, above me, inside me. He was real. I shuddered. The last words I heard him say came back to me: "I promise you'll see me again." He promised. Suddenly at that moment, I knew it was true. I didn't know how or where; I didn't even know how I knew, but I was sure. Something in his voice when he'd said it, something about the way women looked at him, something made my blood run cold. I would see him again. I smiled at the knowledge that frightened me and wiped a tear from my cheek.

The afternoon finally ended. I left behind a desk full of unfinished work and walked out into the sunlight. I sat in my car, my eyes unfocused, for a long time while everyone else left the parking lot. My hands dropped from the steering wheel to rest on my stomach. I felt the new life stirring inside me. After a moment, I turned the key in the ignition and drove home.

hen I answer the phone, it is some guy from New York, from some record label. He asks to speak to Linda, of course. It is her house where I am; she is the person throwing this party. The chair that I'm sitting in is very comfortable and it's a great effort to get up, but I set down the phone and do just that. From the bottom of the stairs, I yell Linda's name, but it is too loud upstairs, people talking and music blaring, for anyone to hear me. I realize that I'm going to have to walk upstairs to find her. I don't want to, but I resign myself to it, when just at that moment, two young girls appear at the top of the stairs, on their way down.

"Would you go get Linda?" I ask. "Tell her there's a phone call from New York."

They are eager to help, and I am grateful not to have to go upstairs into that mass of people and noise. I don't like parties. The only reason I am here at all is to meet Todd, my girlfriend Christine's nephew. We are going to drive over to the theatre to see the new play she is in. This is where Todd wanted to meet.

I watch a small black cat with white splotches on its face dart out of the way of several newcomers to the party. They bustle past me without acknowledging my presence and start up the stairs. The cat, whose name I cannot recall, scrambles under the couch and emerges in the window behind it. The window curtains begin to sway and shift as the cat starts to climb them from behind. I smile. I like this cat.

I walk outside into the cold night air. My breath condenses into a little cloud that quickly dissipates. The snow along the curb and in the street is soot black. A car, the only moving object I see, slowly approaches the corner from a side street. It stops for a moment, and then tentatively moves out onto the main street, turning left, away from me. The car moves very slowly, as if its driver is unused to snow and is afraid. I watch the taillights fade into the distance.

When I look back, I see Todd across the street. He is wearing blue jeans and a black leather jacket. He smiles and waves at me, then jogs across the snow-covered street. I have met Todd before. He is a bright, friendly kid, though he comes across as cocky and self-assured as only someone in their early twenties can. He is half-Chinese or half-Japanese or something. His black hair is cropped short, and he wears wire rimmed glasses.

Todd is disappointed that we will not be staying at the party for a while, but it is already ten minutes after the time I wanted to leave. I live by a very precise schedule. I am never late for anything. If you are late to the theatre, they don't let you in.

I lead Todd around the side of the building to the back parking lot. Despite the windows being closed, we can hear the pounding beat of the music from the party upstairs. Todd talk-sings along with the music. I don't recognize the song. The snow in the parking lot has been packed down by the cars and people who have driven and walked on it. It crunches under our feet. I stop, disoriented for a moment, as I look for my car. I see a car that I think is mine. Icicles hang from its front bumper; snow covers its roof and windshield. "Here it is," I tell Todd. When I get closer, I notice the car sports out-of-state plates; I don't know how I've mistaken it for mine. It's the same color, but I've only been parked here for a short time, so my car wouldn't be covered in snow. It's not snowing tonight.

"I parked in the street," I say as though I have just remembered it, which, in fact, I have. And there is my car parked next to the curb. We must have walked right past it when we came around the building. I'm not sure why I feel so disoriented and out of sorts , but the feeling continues when we reach my car, and I climb in the passenger side while Todd slides in behind the wheel. Todd pulls into the parking lot and the wheels start to spin in the snow. He grins maniacally as he presses down the accelerator and cranks the steering wheel to one side. We begin to slide around in a circle, throwing up a cloud of snow.

"Here, I'll drive," I say. "I bought this car brand new a year ago and no one has ever driven it except me. I'm not about to let you be the first," I tell him.

Todd grins stupidly, and shakes his head no. He wants to drive. The car keeps sliding around wildly in the parking lot. I'm amazed that we do not crash into one of the parked cars. I slap Todd backhanded on the side of his head. He quits smiling and stares at me, his glasses askew. But he refuses to give up the driver's seat.

Todd reclines the seat back almost as far as it will go, nearly horizontal. Although he cannot see in front of us, he maneuvers the car onto the street, into traffic. I grab the steering wheel as he does not see the oncoming truck. "Pass me the bottle," Todd yells. I have no idea what he's talking about.

I switch off the ignition and pull out the keys. Todd sits up, indignant. I open the door and step out. Leaning into the car I finally manage to convince Todd that he needs to get out and trade places with me. "We've got to leave right now, so we can make it to the play," I say. When he opens the driver's door and climbs out, I push down the lock button on the passenger door and shut it.

Todd and I pass each other in front of the car. He averts his eyes, looking up at the low, dark clouds. He will not look at me. I get in the car, turn the key in the ignition and start the engine. Todd tries opening the passenger side door but finds it locked. He wraps his knuckles on the window and gestures that I should open the door for him. Maybe he thinks I locked the door by accident when I got out. I shift the car into gear and pull away. I look in the rear-view mirror and see Todd standing in the middle of the street watching me as I drive away.

Christine will be upset when she finds out that I left Todd behind, until I explain to her what a jerk he was being.

11. Robin and Thorwald

Throwald
he two men moved silently through the forest. They were not hunting, pursuing, or being pursued. Their silent movement among the trees was natural, done without a conscious thought. It was simply their way and had been for many years.

The trail the two men walked paralleled a river on its right bank. The river gurgled and sparkled in the afternoon sun, flowing steadily to the northeast.

Birds—larks and sparrows—flew from one tree to another and back again and sang all around the men. A sudden rustling in the underbrush attracted the men's attention to the forest side of the path, but the animal, whatever it may have been, departed unseen. Across the river, a doe and two fawns approached the water's edge and drank cautiously. The mother glanced warily about. The second of the two men, much taller than the first, idly wondered if he could still bring the deer down with one shot, one arrow. He was sure that his companion could.

The trail they followed veered slightly to their right and widened, a stand of trees between it and the river. The tall man caught up to his companion in a few strides. He stood nearly seven feet, his thinning brown hair still curled about his face, and his beard was unkempt. He dressed in greens and browns and carried a huge staff of wood, nine feet long and as big around as a normal man's forearm. The man's huge hand wrapped around it easily. The two walked side by side in silence for a few minutes. The tall man cleared his throat.

"If you have something to say, John," his companion said, "just say it."

John's companion had been leading him through the forest along this trail for most of the day. His long dark hair streaked with gray was pulled back from his haggard face.

His eyes were cold, had seen too many disappointments in his life, but deep within them burned a spark of light, of a hope still to come. A sword in a worn scabbard hung from his left hip. A longbow was strapped over his right shoulder; a quiver of arrows rested against his back. He carried a long branch he had picked up in the forest to use as a walking stick. John knew that he could use it as a fighting staff if they came upon trouble, as they had done so often in the past. Although that wasn't as likely these days. The man's tunic of Lincoln green was worn thin and stained in many places.

"I'm not the one who should be talking," John responded, exasperated. "Come on, Robin, tell me where we're going."

Robin shook his head. John sighed. In times past his vexed tone would have caused Robin to smile, maybe even to laugh. But times had changed. Both men were less inclined to humor than they had been when they were younger. Too much had happened.

"You'll find out soon, John," Robin said.

John let out a long sigh and swung his staff carelessly. A few leaves fluttered to the ground from the branches he'd swatted. Robin looked sternly at him.

"I should never have left home," John muttered under his breath.

"I didn't ask you to come along." Robin's hearing, at least, was as sharp as ever.

"Aw, Rob, I couldn't just let you go off on your own again. Especially after you said this might be the last time I'd ever see you. Besides," he added, tussling Robin's hair with a huge hand, "it's been a long time since you and I got out in the woods together."

Robin nodded. "Yes, it has," he agreed, "too many years."

"And I have to admit," John said, feeling better now that he and Robin were at least talking, "I needed to get away from home. Just for a while."

"Away from Meg?" Robin asked. A smile played about his mouth and his eyes.

"Naw, you know I love Meg. I'm just not cut out to be a farmer."

"You were a farmer before you joined me in Sherwood."

"Aye, but that was, what, forty years ago? It's hard to get used to farming again, to sleeping in a house again, after all our time in the forest."

Now Robin laughed. It was the first time John had heard that from him during this visit, since Robin showed up unexpectedly at John's door at his Hathersage cottage, the first time he had heard Robin's laughter in far too long. His ploy had succeeded.

"John, it's been years now that you've been back to being a farmer."

"Right," John said, "years. Which means that Robert's old enough now to take care of young Robin and the girls."

"Two sons and three daughters," Robin said.

"Aye," John answered cautiously.

"Who would have thought that our Little John would have such a family? Wonderful." Robin's smile was wistful.

John wondered if he had gone too far, mentioning his children. Robin had lost so much. His pain ran deep even after so many years. It was a hurt that would never completely go away. John comprehended it in his own way, but he could never fully understand.

∞

That night the two old friends made camp in a small clearing near the water's edge. Robin shot a rabbit which John roasted over their small campfire. They had eaten fish the last couple of days since beginning their trip.

Robin ate silently, staring into the fire. John worried. He had seen Robin less and less often as the years had gone by. Before appearing at John's cottage a few days ago, it had been several years since he'd last seen his old comrade-in-arms. Had it really been twenty years ago that they finally left Sherwood? That John had settled down with Meg to raise a family and try to be a farmer again?

It wasn't until John had stretched out his long frame and closed his eyes that Robin finally spoke. "The river Trent," Robin said, barely above a whisper. It was the river along which they traveled, the river that flowed past Nottingham.

John opened one eye. Robin still sat in the same place, still staring into the fire.

"Aye?" John prompted after a few moments.

"It flows north after passing through Nottingham," Robin said.

John grunted. He knew that already. More moments passed in silence. John closed his eyes again and listened to the crackling of the fire. An owl hooted nearby. John was almost asleep when Robin spoke again.

"A half day's journey from here, the Trent meets the Humber. That river flows east to the sea."

Despite the long gaps, this was the most talkative Robin had been in the last day or two. To John, it was something new, as well. He knew every tree and brook in Sherwood. He could make his way in Nottingham. But many years had passed since he last journeyed as far as Barnsdale. He seldom left his farmstead these days. He had never traveled this far north along the Trent before.

"And that's where we're headed?" John asked.

"Aye," Robin whispered, barely audible. He said no more that night.

∞

They arrived at the confluence of rivers around noon the following day. Robin's spirits were lighter than they had been at any time since he arrived at John's cottage, heavy with talk of taking a journey from which he might never return. While it was true that Robin had not asked John to come with him, John knew in his heart that that was the reason Robin had come in the first place. The last of his band of followers, accompanying Robin Hood on his final journey.

Both men were thoroughly soaked by the time they had crossed to the north bank of the Humber. Robin pulled his hair back and wrung it, the water dripping on the long grasses. He smiled to see John shaking his huge head, water flying in every direction. It reminded Robin of the first time he encountered Little John, their clashing staves on the log crossing a stream below, and both of them ending up in the water. John grinned at Robin and stripped out of his wet clothes. They lay on the bank, letting the midday sun dry both their clothes and themselves, listening to the water rush past. Within an hour, they resumed their journey, now heading east along the left bank of the Humber.

That night they camped in a circle of stones they came across just before nightfall. "Men camp here sometimes," Robin said casually.

John looked around the circle, worried. Robin laughed and told him it was safe. Robin was the one who had traveled much in the years since leaving Sherwood. John had settled in Hathersage, raising his family and what little crop he could. Life seemed easier to him with Henry on the throne than it had been under Prince John or even the Lion-Heart. John had grown old and content, while Robin had wandered like a man lost, which, John supposed, in many ways, he was.

Robin spoke more that night than he had since beginning this journey. Like the two old friends they were, the conversation soon turned to their old days together, to their time in Sherwood.

"Those were amazing days," John laughed. "Hiding out in the forest, harassing the Sheriff's men."

Robin shook his head. "The Sheriff of Nottingham. I only wish we could have brought him down in the end."

"Aye. Too bad that fever took him before we had our chance."

"We had plenty of chances," Robin mused. "But it served our purposes better to have a live, incompetent sheriff than a dead martyr of one. I think he never realized how he helped rally the people to our side." Robin picked up a stick from the ground and tossed it onto the fire. "Still, I would have liked to have taken one last shot at him."

John sensed the change in mood; Robin's melancholy was returning. In an attempt to cheer up his comrade, he said, "At least you took down Guy of Gisbourne."

"Guy?" Robin looked up, shocked. "It was Scarlet that killed Guy. You can't have forgotten that."

"Of course not," John said. "But we were all your men, Robin."

"'My men,'" Robin replied. "My merry band of followers. Have you heard some of the ballads they sing about you now?"

John scoffed. "Songs. Could they be further from the truth? I was happy in Sherwood—when we weren't being chased or fighting. And lots of times when we were, too," John added, laughing.

Robin laughed too. "Still, it was a strange life I dragged you all into," he said, his mood shifting again.

"No one dragged me. We all followed you willingly, Robin. We all believed in the cause, especially Scarlet."

Robin nodded. Yet the mention of songs and ballads reminded him of another of his men. "Have you seen Alan-a-Dale, John? These last few years?"

John shook his head. "Since King Henry returned his lands to him, I guess he's been too busy at court. To bother with peasant farmers."

"Did we know back then that he was an esquire who'd lost his lands under Prince John?"

"I thought he was just a minstrel."

"Me, too. At least someone benefited from the Great Charter," Robin added softly.

A few minutes of silence passed between the two men. Robin poked at the fire with a short branch. John looked about into the darkness beyond, still not at ease in these unfamiliar surroundings despite Robin's reassurances. Finally, Robin spoke again, "It was a sad day when we lost Tuck."

John nodded. "That it was," he said quietly.

Robin stared into the fire as he spoke. "It was the same fever that took the Sheriff's life, wasn't it?"

"Aye. Sherwood and Nottingham both lost a lot of lives that winter."

Robin sighed, tossed his branch onto the fire, watched it flare up briefly. "But not Scarlet," he said, after a few moments. "I always expected his anger would be the death of him."

"Aye, and it was."

"Dying in battle, the way he wanted it."

"Swinging his sword to the last moment."

Robin smiled, memories of his old friend swimming about in his head. Scarlet had been, perhaps, the best swordsman among the merry band, and Robin's dear friend and cousin, to boot. "I'm surprised he survived as long as he did."

John snorted. "He suffered his share of wounds through the years." Unconsciously, he stroked the scar that ran the length of his right arm. That elbow still ached with the change of seasons, even after all these years and Meg's ministrations.

Robin leaned back against the wall of stones, his feet close to the fire, and drew his hood up over his head. He looked, to John, not that different than he had when they left Sherwood twenty years ago, or even when they'd first met, years before that.

"And Thomas," Robin said.

"An arrow through the heart."

"Poor Thomas. I think he was the bravest of us all."

John nodded, remembering the former yeoman's valor, his dark hair, laughing eyes, and his effect on the ladies of Nottingham.

"Still," Robin added, "I don't hear his name in any of the ballads."

"What did I say about songs?"

"His name will probably be forgotten."

John grunted. "So will yours and mine, Robin."

"No doubt," Robin Hood agreed. "Nothing lasts forever."

Another few minutes of silence followed. John could sense Robin's melancholy returning, and he softly spoke his name. Robin turned his head to look at Little John. With his hood up, Robin's face was hidden from the firelight. This is what the Sheriff's men had seen and feared in the shadows of Sherwood. John smiled at the memory. Robin waited for him to speak. Finally, "Have you ever seen Much in all your travels?" John asked.

Robin leaned forward. "The Miller's son? No. I heard he may have gone down to London town."

"That idiot?" John exploded. "In that city? He'd be hopelessly lost in ten minutes." John had never been near the city of London.

"Five," Robin countered.

The fire crackled. Robin drew designs in the dirt with one end of his longbow. John looked up at the stars overhead. A long silence settled over the two men. John knew where Robin's thoughts had taken him. He cleared his throat and asked quietly, "You miss them a lot, don't you, Robin? Marian? And little Hugh?"

Robin's nod was barely perceptible, and he remained silent. Marian, his wife, had died in childbirth. Their son, Hugh, named for Robin's father, lived only a few weeks. All of Tuck's medicines couldn't save the child. They buried him in the Greenwood next to his mother. Looking back, John could see that that had been the beginning of the end.

∞

The next day they continued their journey, traveling east along the northern bank of the Humber River. Robin was in higher spirits than he'd been since their journey began, and he talked freely to John of his travels in the years after they had left Sherwood. Despite John's questioning, however, Robin refused to speak of their destination or the reason behind their current journey. All John could get out of him were vague hints that it had something to do with one of Robin's previous explorations.

Early the following day, they arrived at the mouth of the Humber where it flowed into the sea. John was astounded by the vastness of the ocean and somewhat disconcerted that it extended beyond the horizon. He had never seen the sea before. Robin stared over the waves a long time in silence. John watched his old friend closely but could not read the look in his eyes. After a time, Robin led John north down a path along the shoreline. They followed this trail until nightfall. The breeze off the sea, the saltwater smell (he could taste the salt when he licked his lips), the crowing of the unfamiliar gulls—all served to make John uneasy. This was a far cry from his cottage and small farm in Hathersage. Robin's words and body language revealed a mixture of apprehension, excitement, fear, and nostalgia. Robin felt on the verge of breaking with a past full of loss and broken hope and looking toward a future still uncertain.

John woke the next morning to Robin's hand on his shoulder gently shaking him. He was awake immediately, sitting up and looking around in all directions, ready as he had always been in Sherwood for the next spot of trouble. But there was no sign of danger. The sun sparkled on the sea in the east. The sky was a bright blue this morning with only a few white clouds far to the south. John looked at Robin uneasily.

Robin smiled, his eyes reflecting that strange mixture of loss and hope that John had seen there the day before. "Easy, old friend," Robin said. "It's time for answers." John didn't know which of his many questions he should ask first. Robin looked toward the sea. "Out there," he said.

John stood and followed Robin to the shoreline. Out to sea was a ship, a large ship, moving in their direction. It was crewed by men who, without exception, were blond, bearded, and large, though none of them quite the size of John himself. Their massive arms rowed the oars that propelled the ship forward. In addition, a mast with sail unfurled rose from the deck. The prow had been carved to look like a dragon or a sea serpent. John had heard tales of such ships before but had never seen one until now.

One man stood near the dragon's head, his eyes locked on the shore. He waved in the direction of Robin and John and shouted a command to his men aboard the ship. John was too far away to understand what was said, but he felt sure the language was one unknown to him. At least they weren't Normans. At the shouted command, the men as one drew their oars from the water. A pair of sailors unhooked and furled the sail as the ship's forward motion slowed. John, startled and astonished, turned to Robin, who was waving to the man on the ship. Robin was actually smiling!

As the ship drew closer to the shore, the man who had shouted jumped off and landed waist deep in the water. He waded to shore, his arms swinging, his large hands slapping the frigid water. Robin moved past the water's edge, the waves lapping over his boots. When the two were close enough, they clapped each other on the shoulders.

"It is good to see you again, Robin-in-the-Hood," the man spoke in halting English with an accent John had never heard before. The man drew Robin into a hug, slapping him on the back.

"And you, Thorwald, my old friend," Robin replied when he had extricated himself from the man's huge arms.

"Come." He led the newcomer over to where John stood astonished, unmoving, nearby. "This is my old friend and companion, Little John."

Thorwald was half a head taller than Robin, but John was that much taller again than Thorwald. The skin on Thorwald's face and arms looked leathery and weather-beaten. He looked up at John, then back at Robin. "Little John you have spoken of much. But this is a joke? Am I not understanding your tongue? He is . . . not little."

Robin laughed.

John reached out and grasped the man's hand. Any friend of Robin's would, of course, be a friend of his. "My given name was John Little," he said. "Robin and his friends decided it would be funny to call me Little John. And it stuck." He grinned broadly.

"I am Thorwald." He looked bemused.

Robin led them up a small hillock, where the three men sat. Thorwald opened a pack he'd brought with him from the ship and offered Robin and John some dried fish and fruit. As they ate, Robin began to tell the story.

"I first met Thorwald several years ago, far from here, along England's western shore, near Lancaster and Wyresdale." John nodded. He was familiar with the names of those places but had only a vague idea where they lay in relation to Sherwood. "His people are from a land across the sea to the east." He waved his hand vaguely in that direction. John looked out at the sea, to Thorwald's ship and beyond. "They live along the coast, and sail the seas, building great boats and exploring. Many years ago—how long was it?" He turned toward Thorwald.

Thorwald shook his head. "Long time. More than seven fathers of my father."

Robin calculated. "Maybe two hundred years ago. Before Hastings. Some of his people set out on a voyage across the seas north of here, journeying to the far west." Robin stretched out one arm and waved it from one side of his body to the other. John listened, fascinated, his food forgotten. "They sailed for many weeks until they came upon land. Their leader —"

"Eric the Red," Thorwald added proudly.

"Eric the Red was the name of one of their great explorers," Robin explained. "Two of his sons, Leif and Thorwald …"

"My name," Thorwald said. He slapped his chest proudly. "It comes from the father of my fathers."

John nodded, looking solemnly from one man to the other. He could barely follow Robin's story. It was an amazing tale, like a fable that one told to children. He concentrated, wanting to remember the story so he could tell it to his own children when he got home to Hathersage.

Robin continued, "Leif and Thorwald journeyed further from Eric's home, a place he called Greenland." John nodded. Sherwood, after all, had often been called the Greenwood. Perhaps this Greenland was nearby. It sounded like a pleasant place. "They sailed south and west. After some time …" he looked at Thorwald, who only shrugged, "… they came upon another land, a heavily forested place they called Markland, which means 'Forest Land' in their language. They traveled on and settled even further south in a place they named Vinland, or 'Wine Land.'" John smiled. Forests he knew. And they had often drunk wine, even in their days in Sherwood.

Thorwald nodded vigorously. "Vinland. I come from Vinland."

Robin continued, "Leif, Thorwald, and their men built a home for themselves there. Unfortunately, Thorwald was killed before they made peace with those who lived in Vinland before they arrived."

Thorwald hung his head and looked at the ground. When he spoke, his voice was sad and soft. "I am named after great man."

Robin clasped Thorwald's shoulder. The blond man looked up at Robin and nodded. "Several years ago," Robin continued, "Thorwald here and some of his men decided to journey back to their native land. They sailed east across the great sea"—Robin made another sweeping motion with his arm—"and landed in England."

"I spend many months," Thorwald said enthusiastically, "sailing around your English islands. Then it was I learned your speech." He grinned, obviously proud. John grinned back at him.

"And that was when I first met him," Robin said. "I had been along the coast near Lancaster when I first saw their ship. It was quite a sight, John, coming across the waves." Robin looked out to the sea; John followed his gaze. Thorwald's ship rose and fell gently on the water. Several men moved about the deck engaged in tasks John could not even guess at. Others stood quietly looking at the coastline or sat talking among themselves. "I even sailed with his men for a short time," Robin said, his voice quiet with remembrance.

John could scarcely believe what he heard. Robin, a sailor on the seas? On one of those boats? It seemed too preposterous to be true.

"Fine days," Thorwald added, smiling.

Robin looked at John, who could now see the determination in his friend's eyes. "After some time," Robin said, "Thorwald left England to return to the land of his ancestors. We made an agreement to meet here, at this place, during this time of the year. I didn't know how long I might have to wait, but it seems some luck is with me still. Thorwald arrives on our first day here."

Thorwald shook his head and laughed. "We have been here many days, Robin-in-the-Hood. We must soon leave. We must journey across the sea while the sun still is warm."

"Then the time of my arrival is fortunate," Robin said. "You still intend to return to Vinland?"

"Yes. I have been for months in the land of my fathers. But Vinland is my home. Many new men come with me." He waved a hand at his ship. John looked out across the sea, though the sun's reflection hurt his eyes. He could not look at the water for long.

"Then my luck is better than I thought, our arriving here when we did," Robin said. "You see, John, I am going with Thorwald to Vinland."

"What? And leave England?"

Robin nodded. "Yes. There is nothing for me here now. I said my last goodbyes to Marian and Hugh in Sherwood before coming to see you, John. Thorwald has told me many things about the people of Vinland. They're a plain people; they lead simple lives. They hunt deer with bows like our own. There are no sheriffs, no kings. No one 'owns' the land or the deer. I plan to live out my final days with them."

John nodded. The three men remained silent for a long time, as John absorbed all he'd been told. He'd never seen the sea before today. Never seen people like Thorwald and his men. Never knew or even imagined another land across the sea. When he finally looked up at Robin, tears welled in his eyes, and flowed over his cheeks. He sniffled. "So this is goodbye."

Robin nodded. "I'm glad you came along on this final journey, John. You were the first and the last. My oldest and dearest friend."

The two men stood and for a moment merely looked at one another. Then John crushed Robin to his chest with his massive, muscled arms. Robin slapped John on the back. "Kiss Meg once for me," Robin said. "And take good care of yourself, my friend."

Robin stood back and brushed a tear from his own cheek before turning away.

∞

Later that day, John stood at the water's edge for a long time. His eyes carefully followed the boat with the carved dragon on its prow until it vanished from his sight, sailing northward. Tears flowed freely down his face as he stood alone on the shore, witnessing the final departure of his oldest friend and mentor. He looked out over the waters of the sea long after the boat could no longer be seen. The sun was near the horizon behind him when he finally turned away from the sea and started walking inland. "I hope I can remember the way home," he muttered to himself.

12. Sarah

R ydal woke early. It was the morning of Festival Day. He rolled off his cot, then climbed down the wooden ladder from his small room to the common room below. The door to his parents' room at the back of the house remained closed; they were not yet awake. Rydal stepped out the side door where a small enclosure contained the family privy and a wash basin. He splashed cold water on his face, then used the soap his mother made to wash his hair and body. He scrubbed more thoroughly than usual; it was Festival Day, after all.

After he'd dried off, Rydal returned to the common room. His mother stood there, her back to him, hunched over the stove. The circular motion of her right arm and shoulder told him that she stirred something. Rydal paused a moment and watched her. She looked older this morning somehow. She was shorter than her son, a broad, stocky woman. For decades, she had baked bread to sell to the Citizens of the city, and she had eaten her share over the years. She had gained the rotund figure of the baker. Rydal stepped toward her, and she turned to him. The light from the stove's fire lit her face and created white tints in her gray hair. She looked up at her youngest son, who had now become a man.

"Good morning, Mother. I'm sorry if I woke you."

"I was awake," she answered, turning back to the stove. "You'll need a good breakfast before you set out for the Festival."

"Thank you."

"Go on, get dressed. It will be ready when you are."

Back in his room, Rydal glanced around. The room seemed so small, though the only furniture in it was his sleeping cot. His few possessions took up little of the remaining space. It was hard to remember sharing this room with his brother Erad. Since Erad's death from fever four years ago, his mother had become withdrawn. She no longer laughed and very seldom even spoke more than a few sentences at a time.

Rydal picked out his best, cleanest shirt and a pair of black pants. He slipped on a pair of boots his father had given him a few years ago. He had spent the last couple weeks cleaning and polishing them. For a finishing touch, he placed on his head an old, tattered hat he had found in the street one night. His mother had repaired it; wide leather stitches now held the brim together.

Back in the common room, he ate his breakfast of eggs, fried potatoes, and bread. Rydal hoped his mother would make a favorable comment about his appearance, but she remained silent. When he got up to leave, she placed a hand on his arm. He smiled and hugged her.

"Be careful today," she said.

"I will," he replied. Festival was the safest day of the year, but she was only being motherly.

The sun hadn't quite risen, but it had become lighter outside since Rydal had woken. He was anxious to be off. Festival Day came only once a year, and he had been looking forward to it for a very long time. Being a year older than last year's Festival meant a great deal to a man barely twenty.

Still, his mother seemed uneasy. "Remember," she told him, "those living on the other side of the wall will still be Citizens tomorrow, and you'll still be a Worker. Festival Day doesn't change that."

Rydal smiled. "Of course, Mother."

He opened the front door but paused and looked back at the closed door to his parents' room. "Say 'hello' to Father for me. I guess I won't see him today."

His mother nodded. Rydal's father worked as a carpenter. When Rydal was still a small boy, his oldest brother had joined his father in his work. The family hoped Rydal would also, but he showed little interest in tools and wood. Rydal understood mathematics. He knew letters and reading. Those skills were not highly regarded on this side of the wall. There were some who even looked down on those who practiced them. Rydal didn't know what he would do with his life.

But he pushed those thoughts aside. Today was Festival Day. And Rydal was quickly approaching the gate in the wall nearest his home.

He noticed a few other Workers drawing near the gate. They were in high spirits and several waved to him or yelled a greeting. Most traveled in pairs or small groups, but a few were alone like Rydal. The past few years Rydal had gone to Festival with his friend Bix, but Bix's father had taken seriously ill only a few days ago, and Bix had chosen to stay home and take care of him rather than going to Festival this year.

The gate in the wall stood wide open already, even though the sun was barely above the horizon. The guards who normally checked Workers who wanted to pass through, often harassing them about their business, were nowhere in sight. They, too, were enjoying Festival Day. Rydal passed through quickly.

Once on the other side, he heard music coming from somewhere nearby, a tune played on fiddles and flutes accompanied by the beat of a bass drum, but he didn't see the musicians. A group of gaily dressed men and women danced along the street, although not in time to the music Rydal heard. Several of those who had passed through the gate behind Rydal ran to join them. Rydal slowly walked deeper into the city, allowing the sights, sounds, and smells he encountered compete for his attention.

Most of the morning, Rydal simply wandered aimlessly. One need not have a specific destination on Festival Day. He enjoyed the music of wandering minstrels playing lutes and lyres. Women dressed in bright silks danced, often drawing large crowds who watched and applauded. He saw other groups of people dancing, often in complex patterns. Jugglers and acrobats roamed the streets, performing for applause, coins, or simply attention.

Midmorning, Rydal bought a couple of turnovers with fruit jam that he found delicious. For a long time, he listened to a storyteller regale the crowd with tales of ancient gods and heroes. A group of young men preparing for a late afternoon archery tournament invited him to join them, but he declined. He was a fair archer, but not at their caliber. He saw men parade magnificent horses through crowds that murmured approval.

Around noon, he found he could no longer resist the smells of food cooking. He lunched on roasted chicken, fresh baked bread—not quite as good as his mother's—and strips of cinnamon covered apple. After eating, he browsed among the tents where craftsmen offered everything from clothing to trinkets, armor and weapons to intricately carved figurines.

Rounding a corner, Rydal stopped short. Outside a food stall, alone at a small table, in a white wicker chair, sat the most beautiful woman Rydal had ever seen. He barely noticed when someone bumped into him from behind.

"Sorry, mate," the man apologized as he ambled past.

Rydal stared at the woman. She put down the silver mug that she drank from and smiled in his direction.

A sudden commotion caused her to look away, but her smile faded when she did. On any other day, Rydal would have lowered his eyes and walked on, but this was Festival. He made his way through the crowd to the stall near where she sat. He ordered a beer which came in a tall, tapered glass. He leaned against the counter, absently sipped his beer, and watched her. Her hair, black as the night sky, fell just past her narrow shoulders. She had long, slender arms and delicate hands with long fingers adorned with several rings. Could she really have smiled at him?

She shifted in her chair, turning to look at him. Her face was thin, her neck long. Her eyes were nearly as dark as her hair. In the center of her forehead, a faded red scar ran from her hairline to her eyebrows. She smiled again. "Why don't you sit down?" she asked in a voice so soft he barely heard her.

Rydal sat in the chair across from her at the table without taking his eyes off her. "My name is Sarah," she said.

"I'm Rydal."

He drank his beer without really tasting it, although it was undoubtedly the finest he'd ever had.

"When you're finished with that," she said, "we could see more of the Festival."

"Together?"

She laughed. "That's what I was thinking. Would you walk with me?"

"I would love to."

She reached across the table and took his free hand in hers. A plain silver band, simple and attractive, encircled her thumb. On her index finger she wore a ring depicting two intertwining serpents, a common design Rydal had seen many times before. On another finger, a yellow gem set in silver with silver rays spreading out from it represented the sun.

He quickly finished his beer.

Rydal and Sarah spent the rest of the afternoon together. He was nervous at first, but that quickly vanished. Sarah was tall, perhaps even an inch or two taller than Rydal himself. She was dressed mostly in black although her blouse had touches of white that seemed to shimmer and shift as she walked. Simple black and white earrings dangled against her neck. Rydal felt proud to be seen with someone so beautiful. He noticed other men looking at her when they passed; their glances often lingering for a time. She spoke quietly and her voice could become lost in the noises of the Festival. Rydal had to lean in close to hear her. He didn't mind.

As they walked along the streets, she would occasionally take his arm to lead him in one direction or another. Her touch was warm, her tug on his arm gentle. He followed wherever she led. He knew from the start that she must be a Citizen, but it was Festival Day, and he drove the thought from his mind.

In the early afternoon, they stopped to watch a street performance. A group of actors told the story of a band of explorers who ventured into new, unknown lands. Their play was by turns adventurous, humorous, and tragic. Other festival goers stopped to watch, though most left after only a few minutes. He and Sarah watched for over an hour. Rydal knew that many Workers might not understand the subtle intricacies in the story, while Citizens, on the other hand, might find it boorish and beneath their dignity to admit an interest in it. Sarah was intrigued, laughing and gasping, and she and Rydal talked about it for a long time afterwards.

Later they watched a small band of musicians perform. Two men with guitars played and sang, stories of everyday life, stories of love lost and love found. A young woman accompanied them on mandolin and violin. Rydal thought she was quite beautiful, striking really, and she looked and smiled in his direction as she played. But his eyes focused mostly on Sarah, the smile on her face and the affection in her eyes when she looked at him. Sarah had grabbed his hand when she first noticed the musicians and pulled him over to where they played. She held his hand while they watched. The musicians attracted only a small group of listeners, but Rydal and Sarah were both impressed by their skills and talent, the way they complemented one another musically.

They enjoyed many other attractions during Festival Day: musicians, storytellers, food vendors, jugglers, magicians, and more. Rydal was happy to follow Sarah wherever she wanted to go, happy just to be by her side. Her smile was infectious, and he joked and clowned to make her laugh. He lost his heart before the sun went down.

Festival lasted through the night, but finally the streets were nearly empty, and the eastern sky was starting to lighten. A few stragglers stumbled past, weaving their way home. Rydal and Sarah both realized that Festival was over, that their day together was ending.

She hugged him, holding his body tightly to hers for a long time, then drew back, put her hands on his shoulders and looked into his eyes. "I have enjoyed this day and night very much," she said, her voice barely above a whisper.

Rydal swallowed. The nervousness he'd felt when he first saw Sarah returned now that they were parting. "When will I see you again?" he asked.

She laughed the short, crisp laugh he had grown to appreciate so much during the day. "Rydal, you are very special."

She pulled him close as she leaned forward, and they kissed for the first time. A long passionate moment passed before she broke away. When she did, Rydal thought she looked sad, something he had not seen in her eyes all day.

"Farewell," she whispered, and she was gone.

∞

In the following days, Rydal went through his daily routine in a daze, eating very little and sleeping even less. His mother knew something had happened to him at Festival, but she didn't speak of it. Rydal's father barely spoke to him at all and noticed nothing. Rydal continued delivering his mother's bread throughout the city, including to many Citizens on the other side of the wall. He'd often been annoyed when he had to pass the barrier, but now he was glad.

On the other side, his eyes flicked constantly from side to side, hoping for a glimpse of Sarah. His behavior was odd—

Workers were expected to keep their heads down and be unobtrusive when dealing with Citizens—and he was often berated for it. Several times he was struck by an irate Citizen. The blows meant nothing to him, and he continued to search for Sarah among the crowds.

He carried on this way as the weeks after Festival stretched into months. He became disenchanted. Then depression set in. Soon he became morose.

Late one night, Rydal and his friend Bix sat outside, leaning against the wall of Bix's family's home, finishing off the last of a jug of ale, when Bix asked what was wrong.

"What do you mean?" Rydal asked.

"Rydal, I've known you since we were children. I know when something is bothering you. What is it?"

"Can't you guess?" Rydal took a long swig of the remaining ale. He wiped his mouth with the back of his hand and handed the nearly empty bottle to Bix.

"It's not still that girl you met at Festival?"

Rydal nodded. He drew his knees up, crossed his arms on top of them, and put his head down.

"What was so special about her?" Bix asked. "I know you've talked about her and Festival Day, but I never quite understood. Did you see her again?"

Rydal grunted. "No. No, I haven't seen her. I doubt I'll ever see her again."

Bix stayed silent. He knew Rydal would say more when he was ready.

"What was special about her?" Rydal repeated after a moment. "It's hard to put it into words. When I first saw her, I just stopped…thinking. I couldn't see anything, anyone else but her. She's so beautiful, her hair, her eyes, her lips. That's not it, though. There's so much more to her. Everything we did together on Festival Day, everything we said to each other, it all made sense. It all seemed to fit together. I'd never met anyone like her before. It's like I've been searching for someone my whole life without even knowing it, and then I found her. We connected immediately. She understood, she knew what I was thinking and feeling. And I could tell she felt the same way about me."

Rydal held his hand out for the bottle of ale. Bix turned the bottle upside down to show him it was now empty. "And you haven't seen her since Festival Day?"

Rydal shook his head, rubbed his hand over his eyes.

"What will you do?"

Rydal shrugged. "Keep looking."

∞

The next night, Rydal and his mother were alone in their house; Rydal's father had gone to visit a friend for the evening. "Rydal," his mother said, "something has been bothering you lately. What is it? What's wrong?"

"Nothing. Nothing is wrong." Rydal realized that he would never be allowed that answer. First, Bix, now his mother. Something must have been very obvious.

"Do not lie to your mother. You've been this way ever since Festival. What happened that day?"

Rydal sighed. "I met someone. A woman."

His mother shook her head but stayed silent. Rydal stared at the floor while he told her, in different words, the same story he'd told Bix the night before.

"And she is a Citizen," his mother said when he'd finished.

Rydal looked up. "Yes. I'm sure she must be."

"Then forget about her."

"I can't."

"'Can't'? You will. There is no choice, Rydal. You understand the city; this is our life. I was afraid something would happen when you went to Festival. You've always been such a dreamer."

"But why is it like this, mother? Why can't things change?"

"It has always been this way, Rydal. Your father and I grew up in the city, and our parents, as well. Everyone understood. This is the way of life; it will never change. I know you understand that. You need to accept it. As a boy, you were always asking questions, always thinking up stories, imagining things that could never be. But you are a man now and you must live in the real world. Forget about this woman Sarah."

Rydal bit down on his lower lip and sighed. He nodded. His mother stood. She looked at her son for a moment, then turned and walked into the other room.

"I don't know if I can," Rydal whispered once she had gone.

∞

The following day when he returned from making deliveries, Rydal had changed. He smiled and joked like his old self again. His mother silently thanked her gods for his change in attitude, which she attributed to her talk with him. Unknown to her, Rydal had finally seen Sarah once more.

After his last delivery, Rydal headed back toward the wall and the Workers' side of the city. As always, his eyes moved from side to side as he walked, but much of his enthusiasm had vanished. Then from the corner of his eye, he spotted a small group of Citizens on a street to his right. The man was well-dressed, wealthy, and gestured widely to the three women who walked with him. One of them was Sarah. She dressed in black and white again but this time with a red cape to ward off the autumn chill. Rydal shouted her name and ran toward them. Startled, they stopped. The man extended his arm in front of Sarah, as though to protect her. An armed guard stepped in front of Rydal after he'd run only a few steps.

"Where do you think you're going, Worker?" the guard sneered at him.

"I—" Rydal stammered. He knew nothing he could say would make sense to the guard. He looked at Sarah, who stared back at him in surprise.

Rydal didn't see the guard's fist before it connected with his jaw. By the time he had been hauled back to his feet, Sarah and the others were gone. He didn't care when the guard shoved him in the direction of the wall; he simply broke into a run. Before being knocked down, he was sure he'd seen the beginning of a smile on Sarah's face. It was enough to rekindle hope.

That evening, Rydal met with Bix to tell him what had happened.

"And the people she was with," Bix asked, "who were they?"

"I don't know. I really didn't see them that well before ..." He stroked his sore jaw.

"Her family?"

"Maybe. The man could have been her father."

"So what happens now?"

"I keep looking until I find her again. Maybe she lives near where I saw them. I just need to talk to her alone."

"And then what? She's a Citizen; you're not."

"Things can change, Bix. They have to."

"Because of you? I was hoping you would get past this obsession of yours."

"I'll never forget her. I can't."

"If that's true, then I'm sorry for you."

"Don't be."

True to his word, Rydal kept looking for Sarah. Some days after finishing his deliveries, he continued to walk the streets of the Citizens' side of the city as long as he could. He moved as though he had a specific destination in mind and luckily, somehow, he was seldom bothered. He haunted the streets near the area where he'd seen Sarah the last time. One evening he heard a soft voice whisper his name. He stopped and turned toward the sound.

"Sarah?" he asked.

She stepped out of the shadows of a nearby building. She was dressed all in black except for a white shirt, although that was mostly covered by a black cape. She'd been invisible in the shadows.

Seeing her appear, Rydal stepped closer to her, repeating her name, "Sarah."

"Rydal, what are you doing here?"

"Looking for you," he answered matter-of-factly.

"You can't. Rydal, you … you just can't. What brings you to this side of the city?"

"My mother is a baker," he told her, pride in his voice, though he kept it to a whisper. "I deliver her bread."

Sarah nodded. "But you can't keep looking for me."

"I can't forget our time together," he answered.

"It was one day, Rydal. It was Festival."

"I can't forget you," he repeated.

She sighed and looked away from him, at the empty streets. Her eyes were sad. They reminded Rydal of when they parted on Festival Day.

"We belong together," he said.

She looked back at him, their eyes locked. "I'm a Citizen," she said. Her voice had taken on a tone that Rydal had heard before, had heard almost every day of his life, in fact, from Citizens, but never before from her. It implied that this was the last word, the end of any argument he could make.

"I know," he said. "That doesn't matter."

Sarah's jaw dropped. She was speechless. Disbelief mingled in her eyes with something else: Affection? Joy? Relief? Rydal wanted nothing more at that moment than to kiss her.

A sudden commotion up the street distracted them for a second. Sarah looked quickly away, then back at Rydal. "You can't keep doing this," she whispered. "I don't want to see you hurt."

"Is there a problem here?" The voice belonged to a city guard who had approached them from behind Sarah. Rydal had been so intent that he hadn't noticed the man until he spoke.

"No," Sarah answered him, "there's not. This young man delivers bread. I was just telling him what my family needs tomorrow."

"Very well," the guard replied. But he didn't move from where he stood. He just stared at Rydal, eyes narrowed.

Rydal knew he had to leave. "Until we meet again," he said to Sarah and bowed. Then he headed toward the wall, walking quickly.

∞

For the next week, Rydal's mood was upbeat, although he hadn't seen Sarah again. One evening, Bix came over to Rydal's family's home and asked him to walk with him. As they moved through the narrow streets of the Workers' side of the city, Bix said, "I have a message for you."

"A message?" Rydal was surprised. "From who?"

"It's from Sarah."

Rydal stopped, put a hand on Bix's shoulder. "Is this a joke?"

Bix sighed. "I wish it was. No, I was called across the wall today to tend to a Citizen's sick horse. When I arrived at the house I'd been summoned to, I was met by a young woman. She told me her name was Sarah and that she knew you."

"You spoke to her? What did she say?"

"You were right, Rydal. She is beautiful."

"What did she say?" Rydal repeated.

"I don't know how she found me, or how she even knew that you and I are friends. But there was no sick horse; that was just a ruse. She wanted me to give you a message."

Rydal was becoming exasperated. "What is it, Bix? What's the message?"

Bix pulled something out of his pocket. "She gave me this in case you didn't believe me."

Bix held out his hand. On his palm rested Sarah's ring, the ring she'd worn on Festival Day, with the yellow gem and silver rays spreading out from it. Rydal picked it up and closed his hand around it.

"What—?" Rydal's voice trembled and he couldn't finish.

"She wants to meet you, two nights from now, on our side of the wall." Bix explained where the meeting would take place. Rydal clenched the ring tighter and tighter in his fist as Bix spoke.

∞

Two nights later, two hours after sunset, Rydal waited at the appointed place. He'd slept very little due to anticipation and excitement over seeing Sarah again. He'd arrived at the meeting place early and waited impatiently, his mind flooded with questions. Finally, he heard footsteps. Two people approached from the direction of the wall.

A man Rydal didn't recognize drew close. A second figure, tall and cloaked, remained in the shadows a short distance away.

"You are Rydal?" the man asked.

"Yes," he answered, suddenly wondering if he'd been led into a trap.

"You're alone?"

Slowly, "Yes."

The man motioned over his shoulder to his companion. She drew back the hood from her face as she came forward. It was Sarah.

"Thank you, Logan," Sarah said. "Leave us alone for a bit."

He started to protest, "But milady ..."

Sarah held up one hand without speaking or even looking at him. Logan, silenced, moved off to a point where he couldn't overhear their conversation, but could still keep them in sight. Rydal realized that he was there not only to escort Sarah, but to protect her as well. The dirt-packed streets on this side of the wall weren't patrolled by guards the way the Citizens' cobblestone streets were.

"Thanks for meeting me," Sarah began.

"Of course."

"Rydal, you can't keep coming to our side of the city to look for me. You'll get hurt. I don't want that to happen. This must be our last meeting."

Rydal knew he could never accept that. "Sarah," he began, but paused. He was unsure of what to say next. "How did you get to this side of the wall?" he asked after a moment.

Sarah laughed but without humor. "After dark? The wall is only there to keep Workers on this side. The gates would have been opened for us if I'd requested it. But to avoid any unnecessary questions, we came over while it was still light. I've been wandering the streets of your side of the city, to see how you live. I've ..." she paused, then continued slowly, "... seldom been here before."

"How long can you stay?" he asked. He reached out, gently touched her arm.

"Don't," she whispered, pulling away. "I must be home soon, before Father notices I'm gone. I only came to tell you to stop trying to find me, stop trying to talk to me. I'm worried about your safety, Rydal."

"But on Festival Day ..."

"That was different," she interjected.

"On Festival Day," he continued, "something happened between us. You felt it, too, didn't you? I know it wasn't just me."

"Gods," she sighed. She turned her head away, and Rydal noticed a tear flow down her cheek. This time she didn't stop him when he reached up to brush it away.

"I've never met anyone like you," Rydal said.

"And I've never known anyone like you," she answered. She took his hand in hers. "I can't believe this happened to me. I never thought—You're so different than anyone else I've ever known, Rydal. So simple, so real, so..." Her voice faded away.

"You are," he paused, searching for the right words, "you're like the other half of me."

She nodded. "Yes. That's it. If only we could be together."

"We can."

"No." She dropped his hand, took a step back. "I don't share your idealism, Rydal. I can't. I'm a Citizen, you're a Worker. That's all there is to it."

"But our feelings for each other—"

"Don't matter," she cut him off. "Rydal, I'll never again meet anyone like you, I know that. But it doesn't matter. After Festival Day, I couldn't stop thinking about you. Waiting, hoping you'd show up again. But I knew who you were, what you were. Then one day I was with my father, and I saw you again. I started asking around about you, trying to find out more about you, what you did, who you knew."

"Bix."

Sarah nodded. "I found out that you were friends and I made up that story to get Bix to come see me. Just to send a message to you. I even convinced one of my father's servants to bring me here." She looked around at the darkened streets. "I can't believe I'm here."

Rydal stepped closer to her. He reached out and gently ran a finger along the scar on her forehead. "What's this from?" he asked.

"A childhood accident. It doesn't matter."

He rose up on his toes and kissed her scar. Then he sat back on his heels and pressed his lips to hers. She returned his kiss, her arms around his neck. After a brief moment, she broke away.

"Rydal, I have to leave."

Her eyes welled up with tears. Her cheeks were wet with them.

He pulled her ring out of his pocket. "Do you want this back?" he asked.

"No. Keep it. To remember me."

"I could never forget."

"Nor could I."

She choked back a sob, then bent forward and kissed him briefly once more. She turned and ran toward Logan, who had stayed in the same spot, waiting for her. She slowed as she passed him, and he turned and fell into step with her. Rydal watched them until they disappeared.

∞

Rydal sank into a deep depression in the days following their last encounter, but instead of giving in to despair, he became more determined than ever. He would not give up. He would find Sarah again. Sometimes at night, he approached the wall. Rydal knew—or suspected—that guards waited on the other side of the closed gates. He considered trying to climb the wall but knew he couldn't do it without being seen or heard.

One evening, after a long day of delivering bread, Rydal passed an alleyway. It was very late, and although the western sky still glowed, the sun had dipped below the horizon. The alley was shadowed and dark. Rydal quickly looked around, saw no one, and darted into the alley. A pile of broken lumber and discarded cloth sat halfway down the passageway. Rydal wrapped himself in a piece of dark fabric. He ignored the damp, noisome smell of the cloth and huddled down behind the woodpile.

After some time, he heard a guard call from a nearby gate, but he couldn't make out the words. Several people walked past the alleyway on the street Rydal had come from, but they didn't enter. He waited a long time. It was late and cold; few people would be out on the streets.

Finally, he emerged from the alley, the dark cloth still draped over his gray shirt. Cautiously, he made his way to the street where he'd seen Sarah twice before. He wandered aimlessly along nearby streets, looking toward lighted windows. He might have called out her name; he was no longer sure.

It wasn't long before a pair of guards approached him. "Vagrant worker," one said as he pulled the makeshift cloak from Rydal's shoulders.

"Haven't had one of those for a while," the other replied without emotion.

"Come with us," the first one said, taking Rydal's arm and leading him down the street.

"No," Rydal yelled, pulling away from the guard. "Sarah, where are you?"

He felt something heavy strike him from behind, and he fell to his knees. One on each arm, the guards pulled him to his feet. Rydal's head swam as they dragged him through the streets. He barely noticed as they led him down a flight of stairs, along a short corridor, and tossed him into a tiny room, the floor covered with straw. The door shut behind him, leaving Rydal in darkness.

∞

The next morning, he was brought before a city magistrate.

"What is your name?"

"Rydal."

"You were discovered after dark on the Citizens' side of the wall. What were you doing?"

"I ... I deliver bread. To Citizens ..."

"After dark?"

"No." Rydal kept his eyes focused on the floor.

"So you had no legitimate reason for being on this side of the wall." It wasn't a question.

"No," Rydal spoke barely above a whisper. Spending the night on the cold, hard stone of the floor of his cell had brought back some degree of rational thought.

"You were incoherent when the guards found you."

Rydal said nothing.

"What were you doing on this side of the wall?"

Rydal drew a deep breath but remained silent.

"Answer me, Worker." The magistrate didn't raise his voice, but his tone told Rydal that he should say something.

"I was ... searching for someone."

"Who were you searching for?"

"Her name is Sarah."

"I see. And is she another Worker?"

"No. She is a Citizen."

A stern look crossed the magistrate's face. "And why were you looking for her?"

"I need to speak to her. We are ... friends."

"Friends?" The magistrate's tone indicated he didn't believe Rydal. "Do you know where this Sarah lives?"

"No." Rydal could barely be heard.

The magistrate shook his head. "I see no reason to continue this. Rydal, I'm sending you back to your side of the wall. You will no longer be allowed to pass the wall to the Citizens' side. Do you understand?"

Rydal began to panic. He raised his head and looked around.

"Someone else will have to deliver your bread. Do you understand?" the magistrate repeated, louder.

Rydal started to shake.

The magistrate gestured to the waiting guards. "Take him away."

Two guards stepped forward and each grabbed one of Rydal's arms, but he shook them loose and broke away. He ran toward the door, the street, and his freedom. He had only one thought: he needed to find Sarah.

"Stop him!" the magistrate yelled.

One of the guards leveled a crossbow and calmly fitted a quarrel into it.

Rydal pushed the door open and stumbled into the street before he realized that he'd been struck by the crossbow bolt. He fell to the ground. His eyes clouded for a moment, then cleared. He held one hand to his side; blood seeped through his fingers. He saw Sarah's yellow ring of the sun lying on the street in front of him. It must have tumbled from his pocket when he fell. He reached for it with a trembling hand, wet and sticky with blood. The pain in his side doubled as he stretched his arm forward. His vision went black. His hand dropped to the stone street inches short of the ring.

13. The Strange Death and Life of Vincent Van Gogh

T he last time I saw Vincent Van Gogh was in 2008 in Washington, D.C. But I'm getting ahead of the story. Let me back up a bit.

For most people, the first thing to come to mind when hearing the name Vincent Van Gogh is that he cut off his own ear. If they know something about art, they might think of Sunflower, his famous watercolor, or even the Don McLean song *Vincent*. If they've even heard of the D.C. Burning Scandal of '08, they tend not to believe it. I know more of the story than most people. Sit back and let me tell you about it.

For many years, my one claim to fame, my brush with greatness, if you will, was that my best friend's father had roomed with Vincent Van Gogh in post-war France. I first met Steve Sumner during my sophomore year at Cornell. He was a freshman and lived just down the hall from me. He planned to major in theatre and acting, a Midwestern boy who longed for Broadway. My own interest centered on the English language; I was convinced I would write the Great American Novel before I turned twenty-five.

Steve and I liked the same movies, music, and literature. We both collected comic books; he was partial to Thor while I was a Batman fanatic. My Great American novel would be set in an even darker version of Gotham City. In the late afternoons after classes, we'd kick back and watch Star Trek re-runs on TV. We bonded over the genius of Steely Dan's "Can't Buy a Thrill."

Steve spent part of the following summer with me in upstate New York, nursing a broken heart and burning through an ill-fated romance with one of my cousins. During spring break the next year, I visited Steve's home in Minnesota for the first time, meeting his parents, Henry and

Claire. Henry struck me as the supercilious, stuffed shirt academic type I'd come to disparage during my three years at college. Years later, when I'd heard some of his stories and gotten to know him better, that opinion changed. Claire, however, was just the opposite: vivacious, full of life and energy, always in motion, flitting from one project to the next. She was olive-skinned with dark flowing hair and looked much too young to be the mother of my friend. I found her beautiful and must admit to being smitten, my first real crush on an older woman.

It was during that visit that I first saw some Van Gogh's original paintings, although I had no idea at the time that they were his. The Sumners impressed me as sophisticated and worldly, so unlike my own working-class parents, and I admired their art collection without asking questions.

During the next several years, Steve and I spent lots of time together. I ran lines with him whenever he got cast in a show. He inspired me to try my hand at playwriting, rather unsuccessfully, I must say. We admired and/or critiqued each other's girlfriends. We visited New York City regularly, where Steve once saved me from being mugged. We spent a drunken week in Montreal that I barely remember. We'd gone there for a friend's wedding. I graduated with my degree in English after five years; Steve soldiered on as a student for several more.

By the late 1970s, I was teaching high school English at a private school for girls, unsatisfied and bored. Steve was in his seventh year as an undergrad, a self-described professional student. Then disaster struck the Sumner clan; the family found itself in serious financial straits. I'm sure Steve's educational costs contributed, but I never really learned what other factors were involved. Henry was forced to sell several original, and previously unknown, paintings by the great Vincent Van Gogh.

I managed to piece together a version of the Van Gogh story from conversations with Steve and, later, Henry. Most of the media reports from that time and afterward are understandably skeptical and usually flat-out wrong. Here's what I learned:

In 1944, Henry Sumner was drafted into the United States Army and soon found himself headed to Europe. The war ended without Henry having seen any action; fortunately, he stayed away from the front lines. But Henry fell in love with Europe, even a war-ravaged Europe, and decided to stay after his tour of duty ended. Eventually he settled in Paris, where he taught English and wrote short pieces for American magazines and newspapers.

Several months after arriving in Paris, Henry befriended a homeless old artist. He remained vague when it came to details of that first meeting, but he felt pity for the old man. He brought him back to his small apartment and fed him. Henry told me that he thought he'd allow the old man to stay for a few days: "until he was back on his feet." Then the old man claimed he was the world-famous painter Vincent Van Gogh, who was thought to have died some fifty-five years prior. Van Gogh explained that, suffering from a bought of insanity, he had faked his own death for reasons that never became clear to Henry. He didn't believe the old man's story at the time but decided to humor him.

If Van Gogh still lived, he would have been nearly one hundred years old then, but the man Henry took in appeared to be no more than fifty. He somehow suffered little of the normal aging process. After realizing that Van Gogh was indeed who he claimed to be, Henry tried to investigate the man's strange longevity, though unfortunately, he never learned anything that answered that question. Van Gogh convinced Henry to keep his identity a secret. Henry was, to say the least, intrigued and allowed Van Gogh to stay. Henry provided food and wine and encouraged the old man to continue painting.

Not long after encountering Van Gogh, Henry chanced to meet the lovely Claire Corbett. He described their street café meeting in Paris as "love at first sight." Claire called it, "romantic," with a sly smile and a faraway look in her eyes but said nothing more. Within a few months Henry and Claire married and moved into a larger apartment. Henry offered to give some money to Van Gogh "to help him relocate," but the old painter refused it. Indeed, he insisted that Henry keep the paintings he had done while living at Henry's apartment, what some of us later referred to as his "Paris period." Claire gave birth to Steve, their first and only child, and shortly thereafter, the Sumners moved to Henry's hometown back in Minnesota.

When Henry brought to light the previously unknown Van Gogh paintings, the public reaction was just what you'd expect: skepticism, disbelief, the word "scam" got thrown about. Henry persevered. After a year of examinations by some of the world's foremost experts on Van Gogh, the general consensus was announced that the paintings appeared to be genuine. Art's not my field; I don't know how these judgments were determined. But the experts, laymen, and media alike were bewildered by the fact that the canvases used for the paintings definitively dated from the mid-twentieth century. Somehow Henry managed to keep his secret about meeting Van Gogh and never publicly revealed how he'd gained possession of the paintings. Regardless, the art world exploded with the revelation of the paintings' validity. It was the greatest find and biggest mystery of the century. The Sumners collected millions, and Henry and Claire retired to relative obscurity.

As an aside, Henry also owned several pieces of ceramic sculpture that Van Gogh had created in the forties when inspired to try a different medium. Not being able to verify that these were created by Van Gogh, critics and art dealers universally labeled them as "junk" and "amateurish." Henry destroyed most of them, although Steve kept several, and he gave one to me. So, yes, I own an original Van Gogh sculpture.

Another thirty years passed before Van Gogh resurfaced once more. According to Henry, he looked virtually the same as when he'd met him sixty years before. I was working then as an environmental lobbyist in Washington, D.C. Walking along the Mall one day, I noticed a crowd clustered around an old man dressed in tattered clothes. He raved about something, and the throng had gathered to listen with varying degrees of sympathy and amusement. I watched from the crowd for a minute. Despite my particular knowledge, I didn't recognize the man as Van Gogh. He picked up a canvas from a stack piled next to him. He doused it with gasoline from a can. In a series of quick, deft movements, he set the can aside, lit a match, set the canvas on fire, and tossed it at the feet of those closest to him. The crowd drew back, but others nearby, attracted by the noise and flames, joined and the mob grew in size.

The painter picked up a second canvas, repeated his actions, and tossed it onto the flaming remnants of the first. "I have painted these with my own hand," he yelled. "I've been sitting in this park selling my paintings for one hundred dollars apiece." Those words stirred a memory: I had seen the old man before, hawking his paintings to tourists and passersby at this same spot. I remembered glancing casually at them before returning to my office.

"This canvas is worth one hundred dollars and I burn it," Van Gogh shouted, picking up a third canvas off the stack. He lit it and tossed it on the blazing pile, the flames growing. "What is the value of art? I am Vincent Van Gogh. Are these canvases worth one hundred dollars or one hundred million?"

At the mention of Van Gogh's name, the crowd surged forward. Was it admiration for the artist or an attempt to stop the destruction of the paintings? I couldn't say. The old man might have been crushed if he hadn't lit another canvas, forcing the crowd back from the increasing bonfire. I was jostled about. Screams and incoherent yells filled my ears.

Although it had been thirty years, the story of Henry's paintings had permeated the culture. The mystery of Van Gogh had inspired countless theories, books, and television specials. Apparently, no one in the crowd stopped to consider that if Van Gogh were still alive, as I, knowing Henry's story as I did, suspected he was, he would be over one hundred fifty years old. The man setting fire to his paintings in front of us looked no more than fifty or sixty.

I heard the sound of sirens rise above the noise of the crowd. Several police cars pulled up to the curb of the streets lining the Mall. A fire truck moved our way from the direction of the Capitol building. Police moved in to break up the mob and keep people away from the now dwindling fire. I disengaged from the crowd and moved to one side where I could observe. I watched two officers bundle Van Gogh into the back of a waiting squad car. Others gathered up the remaining unburned canvases and loaded them into another vehicle. Firefighters hosed down the area around the burning embers. I watched the crowd disperse and then headed out myself.

Over the next several days, official statements were released, denying any knowledge of the man's identity. The idea of it being Van Gogh was publicly ridiculed. When cell phone video of the incident was shown on national news outlets, Henry confirmed to me privately that it was indeed Van Gogh. Officially, the unnamed man was released on his own recognizance the following day without any charges being filed. The city denied that they had appropriated or retained any of the paintings from the scene.

And that's the last time I heard of or saw Vincent Van Gogh.

At least, so far, anyway.

About the Author

Daryl Lanz was born and raised in Winona, Minnesota. He's lived in other cities, always in Minnesota, but kept coming back to Winona, most recently in 2009. He doesn't intend to leave again. He earned a B.S. in English Education from the University of Minnesota and a M.A. in English Studies from Minnesota State University in Mankato. After a decade working in record stores, and another 15 years teaching high school English, he opened Chapter 2 Books, a used bookstore in downtown Winona where he can be found six days a week. He likes cats and sushi. "Hitchhiking From Fort Lewis & Other Stories" is his first book.

www.ingramcontent.com/pod-product-compliance
Lightning Source LLC
Chambersburg PA
CBHW030328020726
47493CB00004B/1197